villaennet

Also by
ANDY BRIGGS
HERO.COM
Virus
Attack
the nemesis of VILLAIN.NET

WHICH SIDE ARE YOU ON?
Read an exclusive excerpt at the back of this book!

AND FIND OUT HOW IT ALL BEGAN . . .

ANDY BRIGGS
VILL@IN.NET

Dark Hunter

Walker & Company New York

First published in Great Britain in 2008 by Oxford University Press
Published in the United States of America in January 2010 by
Walker Publishing Company, Inc., a division of Bloomsbury Publishing, Inc.
Visit Walker & Company's Web site at www.bloomsburykids.com

For information about permission to reproduce selections from this book, write to
Permissions, Walker & Company, 175 Fifth Avenue, New York, New York 10010

Library of Congress Cataloging-in-Publication Data
Briggs, Andy.
Dark Hunter / Andy Briggs.
p.   cm.   — (Villain.net)
Summary: In a desperate attempt to reunite with his family, teenaged
bully Jake Hunter reluctantly downloads another batch of supervillain powers
and soon finds himself kidnapping the president of the United States.
ISBN-13: 978-0-8027-9498-7 • ISBN-10: 0-8027-9498-X
[1. Superheroes—Fiction. 2. Good and evil—Fiction. 3. Bullies—Fiction.
4. Adventure and adventurers—Fiction.] I. Title.
PZ7.B76528Dar 2010   [Fic]—dc22   2009007463

Printed in the U.S.A. by Quebecor World Fairfield, Pennsylvania
2 4 6 8 10 9 7 5 3 1

All papers used by Walker & Company are natural, recyclable products
made from wood grown in well-managed forests. The manufacturing processes
conform to the environmental regulations of the country of origin.

VILLAIN.NET is used in this work as a fictitious domain name. Walker & Company
and OUP take no responsibility for any actual Web site bearing this name.

For Pete—
a hero's hero . . .
and a villain's villain!

From: Andy Briggs
To: VILLAIN.NET readers everywhere
Subject: Careful on the Web!

As you know, the Internet is a brilliant
invention, but you need to be careful
when using it in your plans for world
domination . . . or just doing homework.

In this book, the villains (and heroes!)
download their powers from different Web
sites. But VILLAIN.NET and HERO.COM don't
really exist. :-(I thought them up when I
was dreaming about how cool teleportation
would be. The idea for VILLAIN.NET suddenly
came to me—especially the scene when Jake
hijacks . . . Oh wait! You haven't read it
yet, so I'd better not spoil it! :-)
Anyway, I began writing and before I knew
it, the idea had spiraled into HERO.COM
as well. But I made up all of the Internet
stuff. None of it is really out there on
the Web, unfortunately.

Here are my cool tips for safe surfing on
the Web: keep your identity secret (like
all heroes do); stick to safe Web sites;
make sure a parent, teacher, or guardian
knows that you're online; don't bully
anyone else—that's seriously not good—
and if anyone ever sends you anything that
makes you feel uncomfortable, don't reply,
and tell an adult you trust.

I do have my own Web site, and it's totally
safe: **www.heroorvillainbooks.com**

Be safe out there!

:-)

CONTENTS

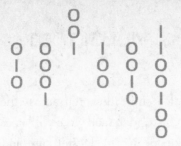

The Great Escape

WHAM! Jake's head jerked back with the powerful blow to his cheek. He had a metallic taste in his mouth: his lip must be bleeding. Through a swollen eye he looked at Chameleon sitting across the table.

The superhero had been interrogating Jake since he'd arrived at Diablo Island Penitentiary, three . . . four weeks ago? Maybe more—days had blurred into one another.

Chameleon motioned for the heavy Enforcer to stop hitting the boy. The man was huge, dressed in the uniform worn by the United Nations' secret army whose mission was to conceal superheroes from public awareness and to capture supervillains. Like Jake.

"Had enough, Hunter?" said Chameleon.

Jake glared at the young man across the table, who was dressed in immaculate black and sporting a sharp haircut with a widow's peak. Chameleon could shapeshift, but this seemed to be his normal form.

"When I get out of here," Jake said through cracked lips, "I'll kill you."

A ghost of a smile flickered across the hero's face. "Fine. But you understand you will *never* get out of here. The outside world doesn't care and your family have forgotten you *ever* existed."

Jake tried to lunge forward, but he was bound to the chair and feeling weak because he hadn't been able to download powers from Villain.net. Those superpowers kept him alive. Whatever powerless replacement Chameleon was pumping into him was doing nothing more than keeping him tired and weak.

"I saved your family," continued the hero. "They will no longer have the heartbreak of suffering such an insolent son as you."

Jake jerked futilely in the chair and the Enforcer raised a threatening hand to strike again, but pulled away when Chameleon gave a slight shake of the head. The hero had never physically struck Jake during the interrogations, but he was more than happy to allow the Enforcers to be heavy-handed.

"I'll get them back," spat Jake. "Then I'll kill you and all your little superfriends when I tear this place apart!"

Chameleon smiled, and Jake wanted to rip his smug face off.

"Your family is gone, Hunter. And restoring their memories is not a power that even you possess." He paused. "I think by now I'm starting to believe you don't know the location of the Council of Evil."

The Great Escape

The Council of Evil was a dedicated group of supervillains who had created an empire in retaliation to the Hero Foundation. Classic evil versus good. Both sides had started recruiting heroes and villains through Hero.com and Villain.net, and both sides had successfully hidden their headquarters away from the other.

"I've never been," growled Jake. "And if I had, I'd slaughter them too! Basilisk did this to me, made me dependent on that stupid Web site!"

"He did more than that, Hunter, and you know it. Your body has become entangled with Villain.net. And that's what makes you valuable to both sides."

"I told you before: I don't care!"

"You have the unique ability to absorb powers from Villain.net, far greater than experts previously thought was possible. But not only that, you can create new ones that we've never seen before."

Jake laughed. This was the usual sermon from Chameleon, but it didn't change the fact that Jake had been tied to a chair every day and beaten for information.

Chameleon leaned forward, tenderness flashing across his face. "Hunter . . . Jake, please. Work with us, not against us. Use your abilities to help the Hero Foundation. Together we can eradicate evil and make the world a much better place."

Jake took a moment to contemplate Chameleon's

offer, but it was a simple decision—there was only one important person. Himself.

With the limited movement available to him, Jake twisted his hand and threw an obscene gesture and a charming smile.

The look of fury on the hero's face was worth the punch across the face from the Enforcer.

The silence was so deep that Jake could hear the blood pounding in his ears. He'd been mentally counting the minutes since they had thrown him back into his cell. The lighting was so intentionally bright that it was impossible to tell where the floor met the walls, and it hurt Jake's eyes and made his photosensitive skin tingle unpleasantly. Aside from his addiction to Villain.net, that was another side effect of his DNA being entangled with the super-power system.

Jake was now feeling stronger than he had been when Chameleon had first apprehended him on the beach of Basilisk's volcanic island. Perhaps there was something in the replacement power they'd been using to keep him alive. But now Jake had had enough. His craving for superpowers was too strong. It didn't matter what the powers were—they always made him feel stronger and more alive. And his body was a cauldron of hyperenergy, sloshing it all around to give him useful if unexpected powers. Most of the time.

He had decided it was time to leave.

On his first night on Diablo Island he had found a cell phone tucked under the pillow in his chamber. On it was a link to access the Villain.net Web site, and he knew from past experience that he could download limited powers from this device. But he had resisted using the phone in case it was some kind of trap set up by Chameleon.

The second night he had received a text message on the phone telling him not to delay escaping. The message was just signed "Your Caring Benefactor."

He had no idea who that person was. He'd speculated it could be Basilisk, who had claimed they were now genetic twins, *almost* clones. But why would the arch-fiend help? Jake had sworn revenge after he'd made him addicted to Villain.net.

Now, as midnight approached and the Enforcers who patrolled the cellblock had returned to their barracks for a scheduled break, Jake pulled the cell phone from under his pillow and stared at the screen. His fingers trembled, both from excitement at the prospect of escaping, and from a lack of strength. He pushed the control pad to highlight the Villain.net link, a lengthy mixture of foreign alphabets and numbers, and clicked on it.

Within seconds the screen changed to a miniature version of the Web site. There was a list of icons, all representing superpowers and all too small to identify . . .

He blindly chose several powers and saw a thin tendril warp out of the screen and tap him on the forehead. Then a sensation like pins and needles rippled through his body and he went from being weak and lethargic to feeling as if he could conquer the world.

Jake leaped off his bed and stretched his arms, feeling the blood flow to his muscles and his mind sharpen to primeval alertness. He had gleaned a little information from the Enforcer guards who escorted him to and from his cell each day. They had talked freely, assuming that Jake was no longer a threat. His cell walls were a few feet thick, and at the end of the corridor, which was lined with security cameras, lay an open courtyard where some prisoners were permitted to exercise, although Jake had never been allowed outside. He was being housed in the minimal security wing; after all, he was now just a boy with no superpowers. Hardly a threat to Diablo Island Penitentiary—the very name of which made seasoned supervillains tremble.

Jake tucked the phone into his jeans pocket—the same worn black jeans he'd been wearing for weeks. He knew that the moment the alarms were triggered, hundreds of heavily armed Enforcers would be upon him,

The Great Escape

and he wasn't sure he had the strength to fight them all. The situation called for a tactical approach.

His fingers traced the edges of the cell door in the hope he could find a gap, but it was made with such precision it could have been airtight. Jake was beginning to think he'd have to resort to brute force when the lock suddenly clicked open as he moved his hand across it. Puzzled, Jake gently pulled the door open and stepped out into the dark corridor beyond. He experimentally waved his hand across the lock several times and each time it slid back and forth through some kind of telekinesis.

"Now that's cool," Jake murmured to himself, shutting the door behind him.

He looked around the corridor and immediately identified three surveillance cameras. He wafted his hand like he was swatting a fly, and all three cameras quickly snapped aside, as if he'd physically struck them.

Jake stealthily approached the double security doors ahead, his mind running through his options. His overwhelming urge was to find Chameleon, who he knew was somewhere on the island, and exact his revenge. But the new cautious side of Jake's mind urged him to flee as quickly as possible. He might have superpowers, but nobody had yet managed to escape from Diablo Island, as he was constantly reminded.

As he took several more steps to freedom the double

doors suddenly gave a loud beep and began to slide apart—somebody was coming in! Evidently he had miscounted while lying in his cell, and this was the scheduled security patrol. Fighting panic, he moved into the shadows—and felt a sensation just like falling into water. He gave a startled yelp as he saw his body transform and disappear into the pool of blackness. His head popped from the shadows on the floor, just enough to comprehend he had become part of them. Two Enforcers had entered, weapons cradled in their arms. They walked past Jake without noticing him, both doing bad impressions of a TV comedian they had just been watching.

Jake gave silent thanks that, by chance, he had the right powers to slide him out unnoticed. Then a second thought hit him—perhaps his mysterious benefactor had ensured that he'd downloaded exactly the powers he'd need, just like Basilisk had done before.

Basilisk. Again that name brought a wave of anger. Jake was sure that he wanted to kill the villain on sight, and he figured Basilisk realized this. The fiend was responsible for ruining his life, getting him imprisoned—everything that was bad in Jake's life had been a direct consequence of Basilisk's involvement. But if it wasn't Basilisk helping him out, then who could it possibly be?

His benefactor's identity would have to wait until he got clear of Diablo Island. In fact, he had no idea where

The Great Escape

the island was located geographically. He clambered out of the shadows, as easily as pulling himself out of a swimming pool, and ran through the doors just as they were closing.

He was outside for the first time in days, standing in a courtyard half the size of a football field. The first thing that struck him was the intense cold and heavy falling snow. It felt like being back in Moscow again. The second thing he noticed was that it was night, but the courtyard was bathed in brilliant floodlights. An alarm suddenly sounded.

An Enforcer in a watchtower had opened the door for his two colleagues to enter the minimum-security wing, and he had watched them step inside without incident. When he looked at his bank of monitors to confirm they were safely inside, he was surprised to see that the images coming from the corridor showed blank walls. He tore his gaze from the screen and back into the courtyard in time to see Jake run out. The doors closed behind the boy, and the Enforcer punched a bright-red alarm button.

"Aw, geez," Jake groaned as the sound of whooping sirens erupted across the complex. This was exactly what he wanted to avoid. He shielded his eyes from the floodlights and saw an Enforcer aim his gun.

"On the ground now or I'll open fire!" yelled the guard.

Jake reacted on impulse and extended his hands, hoping something spectacular would happen. He wasn't disappointed.

An enormous energy sphere formed between both hands and he lobbed it like a bowling ball. The energy sphere smashed into the legs of the watchtower, tearing two of the steel supports away. The entire structure toppled over with a wail of stressed steel. The tower struck a wall halfway up its length, and the momentum pitched the Enforcer hard to the floor.

More guards ran from doors opposite Jake, and he heard the doors to the minimum-security wing begin to rumble open behind him. He spun around and formed another energy sphere—slamming it into the door with such force that the steel buckled, preventing it from opening any farther.

By the time he turned back around to see the growing army of angry Enforcers, a hail of bullets had impacted inches from him—all stopped by a translucent energy shield that expanded from his body and rippled with each hit. Jake was not sure how long the shield would last—the number of bullets increased with such ferocity that he was soon facing a wall of lead. It obscured his view like insects on a car windshield. The clatter of falling shells was almost as loud as the gunshots.

Jake walked forward, but the weight of the bullets made it feel like he was walking through molasses. He blindly lobbed another energy sphere. It must have struck some Enforcers as the gunfire abated and he heard screams.

A voice echoed around from the prison's PA system. "Jake Hunter, you have been identified and will be terminated if you do not surrender!"

Yeah, great options, thought Jake.

With no more bullets ricocheting into his shield, he had a clear view of his attackers. He unleashed another energy sphere and bowled over eight of them, but another ten stepped up to replace them. Movement to the side got his attention—yet more Enforcers running along the yard's walls. Above them all, multiple electrical bolts randomly pulsed from massive spherical Tesla towers dotted along the walls, looking like rejects from an old black-and-white Frankenstein movie. The pulses formed crisscrossing energy strands like a net. His Enforcer wardens had told him that Diablo Island was a "no-fly zone"—the shield was only deactivated when official aircraft visited the island. It ensured prisoners could not simply fly away.

Jake bolted for the fallen watchtower, and once again the Enforcers opened fire. He had a good head start, so he climbed up the lattice tower, up onto its sloping side. Sparks kicked up around his feet as bullets struck, but he ignored them and ran up the angled girder.

As he gained some height he could see that he was

close to the edge of a wide island. Snow and darkness cloaked the horizon, but he could see black ocean waters beyond the final wall. His improvised escape plan was derailed when he saw an Enforcer on the wall carrying a huge weapon, so heavy that it sat on a pneumatic arm that was strapped to his chest to ease the weight. When he fired, a massive blast of white plasma tore the watchtower in two and hit Jake like a wrecking ball.

He was flung over the yard wall, smashing into the stone outer courtyard beyond. The top of the watchtower was blown away and tumbled to the ground with him, burning as it smashed against the stone floor—forcing the men on duty in the courtyard to scatter for cover.

Jake's entire body felt like one big bruise, but he knew he didn't have time to be injured. An Enforcer was running over to him on the assumption he'd been knocked unconscious. Jake allowed the man to stand right over him before he kicked out and booted the surprised guard in the knees. The guard buckled and dropped, giving Jake a chance to spring to his feet and tear the gun from the Enforcer's grasp.

Jake tested the weapon for a second. Weeks ago he would have thought it would be so cool to hold a gun, but weighed against superpowers it now felt like a child's toy, as primitive to Jake as a stone ax would be to an army general. Jake tossed the weapon aside and took stock of his surroundings.

Some thirty armed Enforcers circled him, and more filled the yard's battlements. Next to him was a huge Christmas tree, decorated with colorful baubles and lights—completely out of place in this bleak prison. Behind him was an iron gate, beyond which he had spotted a pier that would lead him to freedom.

"You're outnumbered and outgunned, Hunter!" shouted a familiar voice.

Jake turned, anger flushing through him. Chameleon was slowly advancing through his army of Enforcers. He'd transformed into his reptilian alter ego, walking upright and using his long thin tail to balance himself.

"I wouldn't hesitate to order my men to kill you, but I think that would be a shame for both you and the Hero Foundation, don't you think?"

Jake's mouth was dry. Here was the man who had taken his family away from him and forcefully interrogated him, and still he had the nerve to call himself a *hero*. Chameleon stopped, keeping a healthy thirty-foot gap between them.

"You amaze me, how you got this far. Where did you get your powers?"

Jake flicked a glance at the Christmas tree. "From Santa." It was meant as a joke, but at that moment he realized that the holiday was only four weeks away.

He felt a sudden pang at the thought of Christmas without his family.

"Hunter, give up. There is nothing beyond those walls for you. *Nothing*." Chameleon gestured around him. "This is all you have left. Beyond these walls there are few people who even remember you exist. Don't fight us."

Jake suddenly knew what to do. As with all his previous experience with superpowers, the knowledge of exactly how to use them had come to him from out of nowhere. He thought it was some form of telepathy. After all, Basilisk had droned on about his DNA and genes being a tangled part of Villain.net—perhaps the Web site was *talking* to him? All Jake knew was that he had to relax and close his eyes.

Chameleon's tongue extended farther than was humanly possible as he nervously licked his lips. Jake was standing stock-still. His head was slumped, as if he'd just fallen asleep.

Chameleon took a step forward. "Hunter?"

When Jake's eyes flicked open they were bright green flares. He held his arms over his head and his whole body began to vibrate so fast he became a blur. The Enforcers took a wary step back, but kept their gazes fixed on Jake as a green aura surrounded him.

Chameleon suddenly realized what was happening and darted for cover moments before a radioactive

The Great Escape

green shock wave rippled from Jake's body. It was as if a nuclear bomb had detonated. The snow vaporized and every person in the courtyard was yanked from their feet and thrown against the wall. Unconscious bodies piled on top of one another. Some Enforcers were still conscious and had caught fire—they were running in circles, howling, before they rolled themselves on the ground to douse the flames. Enforcers on the walls were blown backward, many falling to the ground below with a shriek. Reinforced windows on the buildings around him *melted* as the pulse reached them.

Jake turned and held both hands out toward the steel gates. The crackling green energy combined into a single mighty beam that vaporized the gates and punched a clean circular hole through the wall.

Jake ran toward it as the green emanations disappeared.

"Hunter!"

Jake stopped at the hole in the wall and turned to see that Chameleon, still in his reptilian shape, had extracted himself from the mass of howling Enforcers and had raised his hands to shoot a fireball. But Jake reacted first and shot out a stream of radioactive energy from his fingertips. Chameleon agilely jumped aside, but stray streamers whipped against his face, leaving an angry red welt from his right eye to the left corner of his mouth.

Jake ran through the hole and out along the pier that stretched into the sea. The far shore comprised icy cliffs, and a huge iceberg floated past the island. But free of Diablo Island's security systems, Jake was able to fly straight up and was soon lost in the falling snow.

The Hunt Begins

Beth Hunter's long blond hair was wet despite the protection offered by her umbrella. She guided her reluctant parents into a music store and began her usual petulant demands for various CDs.

From across the bank of CDs, Jake watched his sister rifle through the new releases, and he grinned despite himself. Ordinarily he would have had to endure her sulking and tantrums, but right now he missed them. His mom and dad followed, trying to limit her choice of albums to two, but failing. Jake felt sick when he saw them, all three smiling contentedly—and completely oblivious to their son, who was just a few feet away.

Basilisk had explained to him that their minds had been wiped by a powerful technique, capable of blocking even the *sight* of Jake. Chameleon had often taunted him by stating that the process was irreversible—all the more reason for Jake to want to make the scaly superhero suffer.

His mother looked straight at him, but her brain refused to see him, so instead she just smiled in an unfocused manner, and then picked up the CD that happened to be in her line of sight.

"What about this one, Beth? It's a three-for-two offer?"

"Ugh! I wouldn't be caught dead listening to them!" exclaimed Little Miss Prim.

Jake laughed loudly, getting a few looks from other customers. He took a deep breath and held back the urge to grab his family and shake them all until they *could* see him. He reminded himself that he was not invisible to the rest of the world—just his family. Their minds had been rewired. It was well beyond mere hypnosis; it was more akin to brain surgery.

A massive security guard glared at Jake. He knew he could deal with the guard without breaking a sweat, and could hardly blame the guard for singling him out; he hadn't changed his clothes in days, was soaked from the persistent rain outside, and looked pale, almost ill. If Beth could see him, she would no doubt accuse him of being a drug addict.

Jake sighed and left the store before the guard decided to hassle him. Outside he sat on a wet bench and stared at the shop door, waiting for his family to step out. The street was full of Christmas decorations and lights, and seasonal music played from a shop close by. It did little to lighten Jake's mood.

After his initial flight from Diablo Island, Jake had

found himself utterly lost. He had flown as fast as possible through the snowstorm in a zigzag path to throw off any would-be pursuers.

When he finally spotted the lights of a town, he landed and discovered that nobody was following him. Jake's geography was not great, but even he realized he must be somewhere near the North or South Pole. Further exploration of the snowbound town revealed it to be called Nuuk. What surprised him was that this small town was in fact the capital city of the inappropriately named Greenland.

A quick check in an atlas he found in the local library pinpointed his location. With nowhere else to go, he decided to head home, but not before stealing a thick, warm leather jacket from a man in a busy café.

A deed that got him noticed.

The man kicked back his chair and grabbed Jake's arm, furiously yelling at him in Kalaallisut. Jake tried to pull away, but the man's grip was like a vise. He continued shouting, this time trying Danish.

By now everybody in the café was staring at them, and a mustached policeman was strutting over. Jake wasn't in the mood. He grabbed the man's fingers and squeezed—bones crunched. The man let out a wail as he dropped to his knees and swung his other fist at Jake. Jake jerked his head aside, missing the broad hand. With a swift motion he spun around and hurled the crying man over his shoulder—many feet across the room—where he smashed into a display case of pastries. The crowd looked at the wiry boy in astonishment.

"Yeah!" bellowed Jake. He was enjoying the thrill of the one-sided fight; the old bully in him had been dormant for too long. "That's right! The Hunter is *back*!"

The policeman stepped toward him, wielding a baton. He obviously understood what Jake had said because he spoke in heavily accented English.

"Don't move. I am arresting you."

"No you're not."

Jake slid the leather jacket on, welcoming the warmth. Then he raised a casual hand—and an energy sphere erupted. The cop was hurled straight through several tables, scattering customers, before smashing through the window and collapsing in the snow with a groan.

People scattered for cover as the blond-haired boy strutted from the café. It had been a complete misuse of his powers, and it felt *awesome*.

He continued his journey, stopping several times during the flight, each time wishing his benefactor had given him teleportation powers. It made traveling much more comfortable but was one of those quirky powers he just couldn't seem to absorb into his system to use on a more permanent basis.

During one stop he was shivering violently, despite the padded jacket. He used his radioactive power to superheat rocks to get warm, and another time he stopped to randomly top off his powers from the cell phone, which added a rush to his system like drinking too much coffee. He knew from past experience that powers from the cell phone should be much weaker than those pulled directly from the Internet. But now he found them just as potent and chalked it up to the fact that he was now entangled with Villain.net—and that made him all the more powerful.

It was on this last rest that Jake received another text message from his benefactor, warning him not to go home. It suggested that he meet his guardian face-to-face. Jake ignored it; he'd had enough of being told what to do. From now on *he* was in control of his life.

He flew on, his thoughts turbulent. How could he get his family's memories back? Chameleon had mentioned it was a rare power that had been used to take them away. Memory loss could be achieved through a simple hypnotic power, but his parents had had their entire brains rewired. The ability to do it was a rare power, which meant that it was not available online. Could he use the hyperenergy chemical factory his body had become to create it? But where would he start? Chameleon had told him that he could *create* powers, but he had neglected to explain the rather more important *how*. As usual, thinking about the hero derailed his thoughts to those of hatred: how could he exact revenge on Chameleon and Basilisk for ruining his life? And how could he use these superpowers to get what *he* wanted? There was no good or evil in Jake's book—there was only him.

The Hunter.

Jake liked the nickname that the hero fraternity had branded him with, and he promised himself that he'd live up to it.

He snapped back to the present and looked up as his family stepped from the music store, a bag swinging from Beth's arm. Apparently she had got her own way, as usual. Jake's smile faltered when he noticed a figure trailing discreetly behind his family: Chameleon.

Jake was on his feet in an instant. Chameleon noticed the sudden movement and stopped dead, eyes narrowing. Jake swore at himself: he should have followed the texted advice; home was the first place anybody would look for him. Jake bolted toward a set of doors that led into a mall. His family might not be able to see him, but they could still be injured in a fight.

The mall was packed and Jake easily blended with the crowd. Festive music played, and colorful decorations clung to every available surface. A quick glance behind revealed that Chameleon was following. Surely he wouldn't try to apprehend Jake in public, would he? Jake figured that superpowers were supposed to be a secret, because he certainly hadn't thought they were real until

The Hunt Begins

that fateful day in the woodwork classroom. And if everybody knew about them, then the world would be a much more chaotic place as everybody scrambled to do whatever *they* wanted to. But that wasn't Jake's problem. He didn't care if the world knew. As long as he had an edge, then he could manipulate other people and be in control—that's what mattered.

Jake stopped in a central plaza that was a huge dining area, dominated by a Christmas tree. Shopping avenues branched out following the compass points. Jake took a deep breath. If this was the place he would face Chameleon, then he was ready. He was wanted by the world's governments for buying a nuclear warhead, stealing an experimental drilling probe, kidnapping, and many more infractions of the law—trashing a mall barely scraped in at the bottom of the list.

Chameleon searched the crowd, hoping Jake's spiky blond hair would give him away. He grabbed one figure roughly by the arm, but it was a girl, who yelled at him and shook him off. Chameleon absently rubbed the scar on his face, the injury Jake had inflicted still throbbed painfully. He cupped a small headset curled over his ear and spoke in a low voice.

"I've found him. The idiot came home to roost. How long before Enforcer patrols get here? Or any other back-up, for that matter? I think the boy's grown stronger."

A hesitant voice replied through the tiny earpiece.

"Ah, sir, we have a problem here. In the early hours there was an infiltration in the Foundation's servers."

Chameleon frowned. He hated technobabble and was sure people used it to give the illusion of intelligence. "Which means *what*, exactly?"

"Somebody has hacked into Hero.com and inserted a virus. The whole system's crashed!"

Chameleon gaped like a fish. "The *entire* system?"

"Yes, sir. We're retrieving records right now to see if anyone was online at the time, and if they were, they would have had a forced data flush—"

"Speak English!"

"They would have received a power overdose."

"Is that dangerous?"

"We're not sure. With Hero.com off-line it means there are no heroes available. Just Primes. The Foundation has already begun to move into hiding."

Chameleon's heart sank. Primes, people born with natural superpowers, were on the decrease. And those blessed with such powers tended to err toward villainous activities in search of an easy life and quick profit. Most of the older Primes felt they were an endangered species and when threatened they would immediately go into hiding. Chameleon was one of the few Primes left who believed they should face trouble head-on.

The voice continued. "All Enforcer units have been assembled to ensure there are no further breakouts at

The Hunt Begins

Diablo and have been scattered to guard the Foundation's other key sites. If the Council of Evil gets wind of this . . . "

He didn't need to finish his sentence, Chameleon knew well enough that the Council of Evil would maximize their campaign for world domination if they knew there were no heroes to fight back. There would be chaos on the streets, with only governments and overstretched Enforcer squadrons to try to conceal the facts. If the public ever found out that superpowers not only existed but could be given to anybody, then there would be a civil war as people demanded their right to power.

"This can't be happening," murmured Chameleon.

"But it is," snarled Jake, close to Chameleon's ear. The hero froze as he felt something push into the small of his back.

"Is that a gun?" Chameleon asked incredulously.

"A gun? Why would I need to use one of those? My finger is more lethal than a gun."

"You're not going to do anything here, are you? In front of all these witnesses?"

"What have I got to lose?"

That reply sent a chill down Chameleon's spine.

"I want a straight answer from you: which so-called hero blanked my family's minds?"

Chameleon hesitated. He knew what he said now

would affect whether he lived or died at the Hunter's hands.

"A Prime called Psych."

"Where is he?"

"I don't know." It was a truthful enough answer, especially if Primes were going into hiding—and Chameleon knew Psych was not courageous. But the moment he said it, Chameleon knew it was the wrong answer.

"Then it looks like you've outlived your usefulness," growled Jake.

Chameleon had only one option left. He rocketed up the side of the Christmas tree before Jake unleashed a bolt of radioactive fire. The streamers hit Chameleon in the back as he was transforming into his more agile lizard form. He was hurled sideways into the tree, smashing through ornaments as the branches around him caught fire. He was dazed, but had enough sense to cling onto the tree to give himself a moment to recover.

People around Jake watched with open mouths. At first they thought it was some kind of show put on by the mall staff—until they noticed the scaly lizard in the tree. Then panic rippled out as shoppers scrambled away in a tide of screams.

"There's an animal loose!"

Jake struck again, the green radioactive tendrils igniting more branches. Fires spread quickly as the artificial snow ignited, sending thick plumes of black smoke to the roof and triggering smoke alarms that echoed around the complex. The waves of fleeing shoppers screamed even louder as a sprinkler system activated, creating an interior monsoon.

Jake saw that a little kid had stopped next to him, his mouth open in wonder.

"That's so cool!" squeaked the kid. "How can I do that?"

Jake snarled at the kid. "Get lost before you get hurt."

The boy's mother suddenly ran across, her face a mask of fear. She plucked her son to safety, running for her life. Jake could just see the little boy's grinning face over his mother's shoulder.

Chameleon felt the tree wobble underneath him as overstressed securing wires snapped loose. Then the entire tree swayed like a pendulum. One of Jake's blasts just missed the tree as it swung one way—then pitched the opposite way with such force that Chameleon was flung from the branches. He collided with a life-size Santa sleigh hanging from the ceiling, and the fiberglass decoration shattered and fell into the now vacant tables below—with Chameleon gripping one piece like a life preserver.

Water from the sprinkler system stung Jake's eyes, and he had to use his sleeve to clear them. When he looked up he could see no sign of Chameleon in the wreckage

of the dining area. Jake took a step forward when movement caught his eye. He darted around and unleashed another blast—straight at a mall security guard.

In a fraction of a second Jake saw the nervous man's face. He was retirement age and had obviously been coerced into stopping the rampage. Jake managed to pull his aim aside—splintering several stalls in the corridor—but the blast glanced off the man's chest, knocking him down.

"Get out of here!" roared Jake.

The security guard didn't hesitate. On all fours he turned to escape. Jake was distracted by the guard and didn't notice the hero's attack until a fireball struck him in the side. His energy shield absorbed most of the impact, but it was still enough to smash him through a clothing store window. Again, the shield protected him from being minced by jagged shards of plate glass. Jake fell into a pile of well-dressed mannequins and looked up to see a bizarre sight.

The lizard hero was walking upright, his taloned feet clicking on the floor tiles as he approached. His head bobbed with each step and he seemed oblivious to a Santa's hat that had fallen on his head. Jake saw an intense light erupt from the lizard's hands—and a second later a fireball decapitated a mannequin next to him, and set a rack of clothes on fire. When Jake looked again, Chameleon was standing over him.

The Hunt Begins

"Enough games, Hunter! If we can't find out how you work when you're alive, perhaps we can discover it when you're dead!"

Jake pushed his hands in Chameleon's direction and the hero was yanked off his feet by an invisible force and soared back out of the store and through an optician's window.

Jake clambered to his feet and back into the dining area. The floor was slick with water, but the sprinkler system had done very little to smother the blaze that had spread now through several stores.

He saw Chameleon groaning under a pile of broken designer sunglasses. A sudden feeling of doubt crossed Jake's mind. He hated Chameleon with every fiber in his body, but he still could not bring himself to kill the hero—Jake had committed almost every crime he could think of, but not cold-blooded murder . . . not *yet*. Jake had extracted the information he needed to start finding a cure for his family. Chameleon didn't know where Psych was, so what would killing him solve?

If you don't, he'll hunt you down relentlessly, muttered a dark thought at the back of his mind. And he knew it was true. Chameleon and the Hero Foundation wanted Jake, wanted the secret of enhancing superpowers that was locked in his body. And Chameleon had not even bothered to disguise the fact that he was willing to kill him.

Chameleon pushed a display stand off his bleeding leg and looked up to see Jake slowly advancing. He morphed back into his human form, fear crossing his face for the first time. And fear was something that Jake's old bullying detector locked on to. In the playground an expression of fear on his victims was a victory signal. People were always easier to manipulate when they were scared.

"What's the matter, lizard breath? Finally met your match?"

"Hunter, think about what you are doing! You have untold power we could use to help mankind—"

"And why would I want to do that?"

Chameleon blinked in surprise. "Because . . . you're part of it!"

"All my life people have told me what to do. Every time I rebelled against them I got into trouble. But now, *I am the trouble*. Who can stop me? Heroes, villains, doesn't matter. I'll bring you all down!"

"Indiscriminately killing heroes and villains just makes you another power-hungry thug."

"Then I guess that's all I am."

The sound of distant sirens piercing the crackle of flames caught their attention. Then it was drowned out by a loud explosion as yet another shop unit caught fire. The mall was an inferno.

Jake was opening his mouth to respond to

The Hunt Begins

Chameleon—but was surprised to find he couldn't move. A fine crystal coating encased his body as it spun from Chameleon's fingers. The hero climbed to his feet, nursing bleeding cuts on his leg.

"You may be powerful, Hunter. But you're inexperienced."

Jake tried to move, but found he couldn't. He remembered Chameleon using this power on Basilisk's henchmen in a previous battle.

"Before the authorities arrive, you'll be teleported back to where you belong. Diablo Island, *maximum* security. You will *never* see daylight again!"

Chameleon was nose to nose with Jake, the hatred visible on his face. The hero was so consumed by his own thoughts of revenge that he didn't notice the crystal coating begin to crack around Jake's fist as he clenched it.

With a splintering sound the coating broke away into a thousand fragments as Jake tensed his whole body. His fist arced around in a wide punch that clobbered Chameleon in the face, knocking him down.

Chameleon looked at Jake in awe. "That's *impossible*! That stuff can stop bullets!"

"Nothing can stop me," Jake replied.

Chameleon knew he'd lost this fight, and didn't want to endure any further punishment. He closed his eyes and teleported in a sudden clap of thunder.

"Coward," shouted Jake, furious that his enemy had escaped. But the crystal coating gave him an idea. If he couldn't bring himself to kill Chameleon, then why not trap him, permanently encased in a prison he couldn't escape from?

At least until he felt comfortable with the idea of cold-blooded murder.

Distant voices heralded the arrival of the fire department and Jake didn't want to wait around any longer. He had the name of the hero he had to locate: Psych. Perhaps his mysterious benefactor would help in tracking the hero down? He just had to find somewhere to hide, a place that *nobody* would think of looking.

Jake shot from the ground and smashed through the domed skylight above, and out over the city. Crowds had gathered outside to watch the mall burn. Nobody saw Jake fly into the low rain clouds.

Nobody *ever* looks up.

Invitations

Knuckles and Big Tony entered the school grounds feeling very subdued. In the good old days they would have been walking with the psychotic Scuffer and the leader of their crew, Jake. But those glorious days of ruling the neighborhood had come crashing down the moment Scuffer had discovered Jake possessed superpowers. That had led them to accompany Jake to Russia on an insane mission. He had been carrying a huge amount of money in a case; cash that, as Scuffer pointed out, would be better in *their* pockets. So they had decided to rob their own friend.

A bad move that had almost cost them their lives. And in Scuffer's case . . . well, both boys were repulsed when they had been picked up in Russia by a group of Enforcers and shown what Jake had done to their friend.

Despite the bullies' quiet demeanor, other students still avoided them. And the two boys had absolutely no idea that they were being closely watched.

Jake peered out of a dark basement window. Seeing

his old friends made him sick all over again at their betrayal. They had sided with Scuffer and it wasn't something Jake was willing to forget. They were on his ever-growing list; he'd make them pay.

After fleeing the burning mall, Jake had reasoned that the best place to hide was the last place his pursuers would think of looking—school.

He'd stopped at his house to borrow a few things. He made sure he didn't trigger the array of motion sensors in the garden, planted to detect his arrival. The Enforcers had ensured that every trace of Jake had been removed from his home, including digitally erasing him from family photographs. His family would still be out in town, no doubt watching the fire department deal with the blaze he had caused.

The first thing he did was to take a shower, washing off a month of grime. He hadn't even been trusted with a cloth and bowl of water on Diablo Island. Then he slipped into Beth's room and borrowed her laptop. Of course, with no memory of her brother, she would assume it had been stolen. Walking around his old home brought waves of sadness. Jake fought to control his emotions—supervillains don't cry.

He returned to school that evening, and used his assortment of powers to slip past the basic school security and hide in a basement that was used for storage. He connected his cell phone to the laptop using

Invitations

Bluetooth and then jumped onto the Internet using the school's Wi-Fi system. Even though he didn't know exactly how to access Villain.net, the URL being a complex string of numbers and symbols, Jake managed to access it from the text message on the cell. He was pleased with himself; this was finally a real world use of what he'd learned in computer class. His teacher would be impressed.

The Villain.net banner appeared, and underneath it a string of icons. One of them was pulsing, attracting his attention. He clicked on it and was taken to a bulletin page.

The headline read: HERO.COM OFF-LINE!

Jake quickly read through the story. It said that the Council of Evil was rallying its members to wage co-ordinated worldwide attacks now that there were no Downloaders—superheroes who leeched their powers off the Internet—left. Most of the cowardly Primes had run for cover, leaving the world to deal with the superthreat on its own. Jake was about to click on a link to exit the page when a name caught his eye: Basilisk.

Jake felt his cheeks flush with anger when he read that Basilisk's body hadn't been found on his island and the Council suspected he had escaped. There was a bounty on his head for anybody who brought him in— dead or alive.

Basilisk was definitely still alive? Jake's immediate urge was to hunt him down. But he reined in his anger. His family was the most important thing right now.

After much probing and experimenting with the nameless icons on the Web site, he found a search function that allowed him to track down superheroes. He entered the name "Psych" and was rewarded with an old photograph of the hero. He was a middle-aged man with graying temples and a strong, hawklike nose. He wore an unfashionably high collar and struck a pompous pose. The Web site simply said his status was "inactive." There was nothing about where he could be found.

Jake spent the rest of the evening eating dubious-looking food that he found in the school kitchen and downloading a few extra powers, choosing them at random, and relaxing in the energizing feeling that coursed through his body.

The arrival of students the next morning roused him from the best sleep he'd had in ages. He couldn't risk being seen by teachers or other kids, but he was determined to confront Knuckles and Big Tony today. As usual the two bullies took the same long route to their class, a path that kept them away from the main throng of students and teachers. It was the perfect opportunity for Jake to make his appearance.

He intercepted them around the back of the science

wing, where they were in deep conversation. They didn't notice Jake blocking their path until they were about to walk into him.

"Hello, guys," said Jake.

Their expressions turned from thoughtful to fearful in the blink of an eye.

"H-Hunter!" stammered Big Tony. "Didn't expect to see you."

Jake ignored Big Tony; he was the thick sheep who'd follow anyone. His grudge was with Knuckles, who was slowly walking backward.

"Keep away from me, Jake. I didn't do nothin'! It was Scuff, he made me turn on you."

"Sure. He made you point a gun at me." Knuckles's mouth hung open. "I don't forget traitors."

Jake raised his hand—at the same moment the school bell rang, breaking the standoff. Knuckles barreled through the science wing door next to him. Big Tony hesitated before he followed. Jake didn't move. He couldn't show himself in public and he knew the two bullies would be too scared to mention anything.

Jake just stepped into the shadows and melted away, back to his hiding place.

To those who didn't know him, it seemed that Mr. Grimm had had his sense of humor surgically removed.

Those who did know him were fully aware that he had never had one.

Dressed in his impeccable black suit, dazzling white shirt, and thin black tie—an ensemble that had become his calling card—Mr. Grimm read the message on the display in front of him. He adjusted his square-rimmed glasses and tapped his chin thoughtfully. It looked like it was going to be a busy day.

Mr. Grimm was a fixer. Somebody large corporations or governments paid to solve impossible, and often illegal, problems. He worked for money, not loyalty, and had no morals. Such a flexible attitude occasionally meant that he found himself working for opposing sides at the same time. He was a double agent. And to the best of his abilities, Mr. Grimm always made sure he carried out his client's wishes. After all, that's why they paid him so much.

He stared at the instructions on the screen as he rode in the back of a large black SUV with tinted windows. He had two jobs to perform; unusually they were both at the same location, and both for opposing forces. He would first deal with the one that interested him the most: Jake Hunter.

That name had been whispered through corridors of both the Hero Foundation and the Council of Evil. The boy was apparently a key to amplifying superpowers to extraordinary degrees and creating new ones

Invitations

not naturally found in Primes. That was something that Mr. Grimm found most interesting for himself. Mr. Grimm was a Prime.

He glanced at the satellite navigation system and saw that he would be at the school in twenty minutes. He relaxed in his seat and pondered the situation that had been presented to him.

Hero.com was temporarily off-line. Like its counterpart, Villain.net, the Web site was the first and main line of defense against the enemy. Now an ingeniously crafted virus had brought it down, created by the rogue supervillain Basilisk. The Foundation's technicians were scrambling to fix it, and to stop the growing number of villains who were suddenly coming out of the woodwork and taking advantage of the situation. It also meant that each of the Council members was attempting to move into a more powerful position—including his client. It was the usual political power struggle found anywhere in the world—only in this one the participants had superpowers.

There were currently eight members of the Council and the role of chairperson was supposed to rotate regularly among the Council members, but for several years it had stuck with just one archvillain, much to the chagrin of the other Council members. Yet they were so involved in their own machinations that they simply couldn't seem to work together to topple their unofficial leader, or even band together to make a coherent assault on the Hero Foundation.

And between them all stood an oblivious boy who could aid both sides.

Or benefit Mr. Grimm personally.

He closed his eyes and set about figuring what strings he needed to pull in order to look after his own needs.

Chameleon winced as the nurse pulled the final stitch in his arm tight. He looked as if he'd gone several rounds in a boxing ring and *then* been thrown through a window and beaten up some more. He didn't possess the power of regeneration, and he wished he could trade one of his many other powers for it. Once the nurse left him alone in the secret Foundation hospital, Chameleon used his camouflage powers to hide the cuts and bruises—showing an injury to your opponent was never a good idea.

He then left the ward and took an elevator down to a control bunker beneath the hospital. From here, he had communication links with the rest of the Higher Energy Research Organization, or "Hero Foundation" as it was often called.

Chameleon sat down when he noticed the screen was flashing the message: INCOMING TRANSMISS-ION. He tapped the touch screen and waited for a video

Invitations

feed of the Foundation's leader to appear. Eric Kirby was wrinkled from worry, and ran a hand through his white hair. A mustache sat under his nose like an albino caterpillar.

"Chameleon, I must be swift. We are relocating the headquarters in case our position has been compromised. What is happening in your sector?"

"Intelligence says that the Council has been issuing permits like crazy. We have a few Primes protecting London, Paris, Berlin, and New York but we are too short staffed. If you could just order—"

"You know as well as I that I cannot order *any* Prime to fight when our numbers are so low."

"But *now* is the time! If the Council's forces overrun the cities, then how are we to claim them back? And the Enforcers are overstretched due to recent UN budget cuts. If they can't keep our existence away from the public, then you know what will happen!"

"Of course I know! It's what we've dreaded for decades! Their faith in their governments will crumble; there would be a backlash against both heroes and villains, which would undoubtedly lead to protests and riots as people demand access to our powers." The passion on Kirby's face had twisted into a grimace. "The boy. The boy possesses the ability to absorb and amplify our entire catalog of powers. And you let him slip through your fingers!"

Chameleon sighed. He'd taken enough blame for what had happened on Diablo Island. Just because he was working for the good guys didn't mean that *everybody* was nice to each other.

"Events at Diablo were completely unprecedented," Chameleon snapped back. "I would like to have seen Commander Courage there, stopping him." Chameleon winced the moment the comments were out of his mouth. Commander Courage was a pseudonym Kirby had used when he was much younger.

Kirby refused to get pulled into an argument. "I just want to know what you're doing about things *now*."

"We have traced some Hero.com subscribers who were online during the virus infection. There are four of them who received a surge of power. I was going to speak to them personally."

Kirby waved his hand dismissively. "I'm already on it. I have sent Mr. Grimm to talk to them, although it would help if you dropped him a video link to assure the cadets of his authenticity."

Chameleon didn't like the term *cadets*; it sounded too militaristic, but Kirby had old-school values. Chameleon also had reservations about Grimm. "I don't trust Grimm any farther than I can—"

"I do. He's a sound asset. One hundred percent reliable."

"With Enforcer units stretched and most people in

Invitations

hiding," Chameleon tried not to look at Kirby when he said that, "then there is very little we can do. I have heard reports of trouble in America and have spoken to the president and offered my services."

"And the boy?"

"Hunter is in hiding too. And until he surfaces, there's nothing I can do."

"The boy's powers are the key to our surviving this. Find him. Mobilize Teratoid."

There was a long pause. Chameleon had been monitoring the Teratoid *situation* and still didn't know what to make of it. "But that's like using a . . . a . . . " Words failed him. "Teratoid is nothing more than a dumb animal. A shell of what he used to be."

"By all accounts nothing has changed then." Kirby laughed. "And Teratoid has a *unique* tracking ability. Unleash him and assign an Enforcer squad to cover him. He will lead us to the boy."

The screen went blank. Unleashing Teratoid in public was like letting a caged lion run free in a school. Even though the room was pleasantly warm, Chameleon had goose bumps.

Jake tore his gaze away from the laptop and looked around the dark basement. His ears strained against the silence. Minutes earlier he had slipped out to see if he could find Knuckles and Big Tony again. They were as predictable as ever, skipping class. This time they saw Jake first and ran.

Jake had been forced to hide in the shadows as a pair of teachers passed, quietly talking about their Christmas holiday plans. By the time they had passed and he'd made it out to the parking lot, he was greeted by a surprising sight.

Knuckles lay crumpled against a teacher's battered car, the alarms shrieking. Jake had been in enough superfights to recognize the great force that must have hit him. But the only person around was the weedy Professor kid he always picked on, who was sprinting away from the scene. Jake shook his head. Obviously Professor had witnessed something he wasn't supposed to see. The kid just wouldn't be able to understand the world of superpowers.

But that did leave an alarming conclusion—there was a Super loose in the school. Could it be Chameleon again?

He headed back to the basement to gather the laptop and cell phone. He didn't want to lose his only link to Villain.net. The Web site was the only thing that could feed his power addiction and keep him alive. The placebo Chameleon had pumped through him at Diablo Island was no substitute either. He was sure that would have eventually killed him too.

Invitations

"Mr. Hunter," said a voice in the shadows.

Jake whirled around in a battle stance, but didn't fire any powers. Not until he could see his target.

Mr. Grimm stepped from the shadows, offering a thin smile. He clasped his hands together and regarded Jake with curiosity.

"Who wants to know?"

"A safer answer would have been no. Your answer was a confirmation."

Mr. Grimm took another step forward, and Jake tutted. "Better not move again unless you want to be toast. I asked you a question."

"My name is Mr. Grimm. I have a message for you, from your benefactor. An arrangement to meet and discuss business."

Jake frowned. He felt uncomfortable with Grimm's superior tones. "And just who is my benefactor?"

"I'm afraid I cannot tell you that. Suffice to say, they thought a meeting arranged by a middleman such as myself would be safer for you both. The details will be sent to your phone, which, incidentally, is how I located you. Until this evening, sir. Good afternoon."

Mr. Grimm took a step back into the shadows.

"Wait!" Jake ran forward, but Grimm had vanished. Jake threw over a table with a loud clatter, as if expecting the man to be hiding under it, but there was nobody there.

If Grimm had been sent by the Hero Foundation, he would have run in, guns blazing. Likewise, he would have thought the same for the Council of Evil. Basilisk and Chameleon had warned him that both parties wanted him as a superweapon, a fact that just added to Jake's goal to eliminate *both sides*. Each was as crooked as the other.

His thoughts were disturbed by a female voice. "Hello?"

Jake's head snapped around, and he raised his hands to fight. Then he hesitated. Lorna Wilkinson was staring at him with wide eyes. Jake blushed and lowered his hands, guessing that he must look like a complete idiot.

"Hello, Lorna. Great to see you." And he meant it. Lorna was the first person he'd met in a while who didn't judge him. She'd asked him out on a date weeks ago, but he hadn't been able to make it as events with Basilisk had gotten out of control and he'd turned into an international fugitive, nearly died, and then been imprisoned. It had been a bad few weeks.

"What are you doing here?" she asked, looking around to see if they were alone. She spotted the laptop and frowned.

Jake moved so that he blocked the view of Villain.net on-screen.

Invitations

"I . . . er . . . I'm hiding." He thought honesty was the best policy when dealing with Lorna.

"Everybody's been talking about you. You're a hero at school."

Jake blinked in surprise. "What?"

"Yeah. Whatever you did to the woodwork wing has meant we're off school for the next two days while they knock it down."

"Cool."

"What's happened? You've been missing for ages since I asked . . . er . . . mentioned . . . you know . . . hanging out."

"It wasn't you, I just . . . got kicked out of my home." Jake rolled his eyes; so much for honesty. "My dad got a little crazy . . . you know how parents are."

"Kicked out?" Lorna looked around the room. "You're staying here? At school?"

"Just for tonight, till I can work things out."

"That's terrible."

"Yeah. Who'd have thought I'd be spending more time here than anyone else?"

Lorna laughed, then thought for a moment. "You could stay at my house."

Jake hesitated.

"In the garage. My parents won't be using it. If it's just for the night? Then maybe tomorrow we could . . . go somewhere?"

Jake was touched by the generous offer. He looked around the basement as the lunch bell rang above them.

"It would sure beat sleeping here again. Okay, thanks. Just for the night though. And I have to go somewhere first, so it might be late by the time I get to your house. Like midnight, late."

"I don't mind. I'll keep an eye out for you."

She gave him a broad smile, which Jake matched. Then they both looked around awkwardly.

"I better go," said Lorna. "See you tonight?"

Jake nodded. "Count on it."

Burning with embarrassment and excitement, Jake watched Lorna run back up the steps. It left Jake feeling happier than he had been in a long time. The mobile on the desk vibrated, signaling he had a text message. No doubt it was instructions to meet his mysterious benefactor.

CLUNK! Chameleon stepped back as the bulky steel clamps moved away from the giant figure that was pinned to a vertical table. The staff at the Higher Energy Research Organization had named it, after much thumbing through dictionaries, Teratoid.

What was once Warren Feddle, known to his friends and enemies alike as Scuffer, was now a lumbering mass of contorted flesh and rippling muscles. Standing eight feet tall, Scuffer was unrecognizable except for his face, which was puffed and distorted. A dark blue jumpsuit covered his body, leaving his enormous hands and feet free.

Enforcers had found him like this on the outskirts of Moscow after Hunter had used a previously unknown superpower on him. Foundation scientists still didn't know what Hunter had done, but guessed it was a mutated combination of a teleport power and some kind of strength increase.

"Feddle?" Chameleon said from a safe distance. The brute did not seem to hear. Instead he was studying the pneumatic clamps that still bound his ankles and wrists. Since he had been discovered unconscious in the snow, the boy had seemed to have almost no memory of who he was. In fact he now possessed the learning capabilities of a dog. And even with his dubious school record, that did not bode well for Scuffer.

"Teratoid?" said Chameleon. He hated the name, but the scientists studying him had thought it appropriate. Still no response. He sighed. "Scuffer?"

The beast responded with a grunt; his nickname was one of the few things he did remember. "We're going to let you out of your chains, but you must do something for us. Do you understand?"

Scuffer made a gurgling sound and strained against

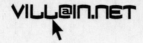

his shackles. They had let him loose a few times, and at first he had behaved. That was until he got into one of his rages and became a wrecking machine. His strength was pushing the upper scales of any Prime ever recorded, plus he had the speed, agility, and peculiar teleport jumping power that made him a deadly opponent. The Enforcers kept a titanium shock collar around his neck, ready to stun him if he got out of hand. Chameleon knew that if the brute ever figured out that it was the collar that was keeping him prisoner he would tear it apart. For now, his stupidity made him manageable.

With another asthmatic hiss of pneumatics, the final clamps released Teratoid and he dropped to the floor with such force the room shook. Scuffer sniffed the air and faced Chameleon with a dopey expression.

"If this is what Hunter can do to his friends, God help his enemies," whispered Chameleon to a scientist next to him. "Scuffer, we have a special mission for you. One that allows you to go outside."

Scuffer grinned—he understood *that*. His true skill was in tracking. The researchers were baffled as to exactly how this power worked, but Scuffer could track *almost* anybody, anywhere. Chameleon rolled his fingers across a plastic box that contained Hunter's blankets from his cell on Diablo Island. There should be scent enough on them to launch the Teratoid.

There would be no saving him then.

Invitations

* * *

Mr. Grimm had created his own teleportation portal to take him and Jake to the rendezvous with his benefactor. It was a rippling oval that hung in the air. There was no sense of traveling, no sickening feeling Jake was used to after he'd teleported in the past. Mr. Grimm beckoned and Jake placed one foot in and poked his head through.

Passing through the portal was like walking through a door. Jake's right foot was on a lush green hill, thousands of miles from the concrete his left foot was standing on. Mr. Grimm stood waiting for him.

"All the way through. We don't want to be losing any bits of you."

Jake stepped completely through.

"Wow. That's a much better way to travel."

"Yes. Portal shifting is much more civilized. Apparently it involves wormholes and bending space and time, but it only allows the passage of a couple of people. It's all very . . . quantum."

Jake took in his new surroundings. They were on a small island in the middle of the Atlantic Ocean called St. Helena. Jake had been surprised, after searching the Internet, to find that it was owned by Great Britain. It turned out to be a green lump over a thousand miles off the coast of Africa.

It was night by the time Jake reached the meeting point on top of Mount Actaeon. Below him, slopes were covered in coffee plantations. From his vantage point, Jake had a clear view of the ocean to the south. It was a perfect place to meet, with very little cover so that neither side could launch any nasty surprises. A pleasantly warm breeze ruffled his hair, and for a moment he imagined that he could forget all his problems.

"So, can you now tell me who I'm meeting?"

Grimm pointed to the horizon. "Your appointment is arriving now." He pointed to the east, where a circular craft soared over the hills. It was black, had no running lights associated with conventional aircraft, and was as silent as a ghost.

Jake felt a little uneasy and couldn't shake the image of a flying saucer out of his mind. But those thoughts vanished when the craft got closer—now he could tell that it was about the length of a bus, with a distinctive triangular logo painted on the flanks, the letters COE underneath. It was a Council of Evil shuttle craft.

"You tricked me!" he snarled. He clenched his fists and flames engulfed his hands like fiery boxing gloves. For the first time, Mr. Grimm displayed an emotion—fear.

"I assure you it's not what you think."

"The Council wants me as much as the Foundation," growled Jake. "That's not going to happen."

Invitations

"I understand. But this is not a Council matter. This is more . . . *political.*"

Three landing skis extended from the Council ship as it landed close by. A ramp unfolded from the belly of the craft, and Jake could hear footsteps approaching. He held his breath and willed every superpower he possessed to be on standby.

"Mr. Hunter, may I present your benefactor," Grimm said with a flourish as he pointed to the ramp.

When Jake saw the figure, he hesitated, his guard momentarily down. This certainly wasn't what he was expecting.

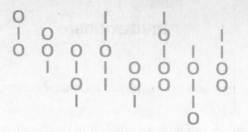

On the Trail

Chameleon crouched low behind a bank of trash cans that had been set alight during the fight. He looked around and saw that three Enforcers were on the floor groaning in pain, another two seemed to be dead. Chameleon himself was exhausted. He had been working hard these last few months and was finally realizing he was burned out. Shortly after releasing Teratoid he'd had to teleport here to try to control a situation that had developed.

He poked his head up and peered beyond the flames. The entire street was destroyed, cars aflame, some lying on their hoods. Alarms sounded from every building. What had once been a pleasant street in Rome was now a war zone, the damage so severe that the government would have a hard time covering it up.

The uncontrolled fires in Banca Popolare Italiana billowed into the night sky, and a figure walked out covered in intense blue flames. He went by the name Inferno—and he was staring in disbelief at the armful of burning euro notes he was cradling.

On the Trail

"My money!" he bellowed in a gravelly voice.

Chameleon rolled his eyes. Inferno wasn't the brightest of villains. But even the dumb ones were making the most of Hero.com being off-line. The Web site was more than a place to download superpowers; it provided trusted field operatives with information on the villains they were facing. Without it, Chameleon had no idea what Inferno's weak spot could be.

He ducked back down as Inferno roared in frustration, shooting a massive plume of fire skyward. He was about to pick himself up to try to stop the villain again when his earpiece chimed. He answered quickly, hoping the sound hadn't attracted the attention of the fiend.

"What?" hissed Chameleon in a whisper. "I'm a little busy right now."

The voice on the other end was a fresh-sounding Californian surfer type, obviously one of the new Enforcers who had been drafted at short notice.

"Dude, I was told to tell you that, like, Tera . . . te-ra . . . however you say it, has, like, lost the *other* dude."

Gunfire erupted at the end of the street as the Italian military finally arrived with a pair of armored Humvees. Chameleon cupped his hand against the noise as he tried to think. He hated the Enforcers' communications systems and had requested they outsource the job to a more reliable company.

"Teratoid?"

"Yo, that's the one."

"He's lost Hunter's trail?"

"They said, like, they'll resume tomorrow. Or somethin' like that."

"That was it? The whole message?"

"Oh, man, wish I could remember." In the long pause that followed, a blazing Humvee twisted over Chameleon's head and smashed against a wall. "Oh yeah, I remember now. Something about that dude . . . um . . . the kid you mentioned who'd sprung from jail. They found a spy at Dibilobo . . . that prison. Spy said he was working for . . . " There was an intake of breath as he tried to recall the name. "Chromosome?"

Chameleon was shocked. "I'll report in later." He cut the communication link before the surfer dude could hear the despair he now felt.

Chromosome had decided to step into Jake Hunter's life. How could things get any worse?

Many things struck Jake when he saw Chromosome descend from the COE shuttle. The first was that she was incredibly beautiful. Just under six feet tall, with long blond hair held tight in a ponytail and the looks of a supermodel—not really surprising, since she had vainly reengineered her own genetic structure to be perfect.

On the Trail

She didn't need makeup; it was all "built-in." She wore a silver one-piece suit with black boots and a metal belt buckle with the logo "XX." Jake wasn't aware that it signified that, genetically, all women have "XX" chromosomes, and men had "XY"—that's what really distinguishes boys from girls.

The second most striking thing ruined the whole illusion of perfect beauty. About a hundred chrome spiders, all identical and the size of tarantulas, scuttled from the ship and covered the ground around her while others raced across her body. Her Legion. Jake wasn't afraid of spiders, and he'd often taunted his sister with large specimens at home, but the sight in this context unnerved him and he took a step back.

She regarded him with keen blue eyes. "So you are the one they all talk about?" Her accent had a South African twang.

Jake nervously eyed the metallic-skinned spiders that patrolled the area but kept away from him. He noticed Mr. Grimm allowed several to crawl across his shoes, although he didn't look too happy about it.

"Suppose I am. You're the one who gave me the phone?"

"Yes. I didn't think a full-scale attack on Diablo was warranted when you had the ability to slip out. My name is Chromosome."

"And you're a member of the Council of Evil, right?

Let me guess, you didn't want the Hero Foundation discovering how I can absorb and amplify so many powers. And you thought that it would be better if I worked for you?" Jake had been thinking about it a lot, and he'd been drawing up his own plans in response.

Chromosome gave him a dazzling smile. "Of course. But don't let my transportation confuse you. I am one of the eight members of the Council. We represent the epitome of evil, so I am told. Think of us as a government, and like all governments, people wish to overthrow us, like your pal Basilisk."

Jake tried not to let his emotions show, but Chromosome saw the anger in his eyes.

"Somebody you no doubt would like to get hold of? He's still alive, you know." Chromosome circled Jake as she talked, always her Legion scouting the ground ahead. "And like governments, we have internal power feuds happening all the time. I sent one of my supporters to help Basilisk bring down the Hero Foundation. She's still with Basilisk now, in fact. Shall I tell you where?"

Jake knew she was taunting him, and he liked her less with every passing second. Jake wanted to get his hands on both Basilisk and Chameleon, but that would have to wait until after he won back his family.

"I'm not going to work for the Council," he said,

tensing because he anticipated a violent reaction. Instead, Chromosome laughed pleasantly.

"Good. I don't want you to, either. I will be blunt with you. I am tired of my fellow Council members and wish to replace them. The whole organization will run more efficiently with a woman's touch, don't you think?"

Jake dared not answer with what he really thought. He glanced at Mr. Grimm, who was staring at him intently.

"But don't get me wrong. This is no petty power struggle. I have bigger, more impressive plans. The Council, the Foundation, they're just speed bumps to my goals. I don't want you working for me, either. You're such an independent boy. Too clever to be a lackey, and too strong for me to completely trust you."

Jake knew he was being buttered up, and he was embarrassed to discover it was working.

"I don't understand what you want from me."

"I want to trade favors. Virtually every established villain is currently applying to the Council for their crazy schemes to carve a patch on the globe they can call their own. With Primes hiding and no toy heroes left anymore, it's becoming almost too easy. My problem is that idiots on my side respect the Council *too* much; they are terrified of breaking the rules. So I can't trust them for what I have in mind. On the other hand you have those like Basilisk." Jake bristled again at the mention of the name. A slight smile tugged the corner of Chromosome's mouth. "I know you are very well acquainted with him. He most definitely can't be trusted. He likes his secrets too much."

Jake felt his skin crawl, then realized that it was because several spiders were creeping up his legs. He tried to shake them off but they wouldn't budge.

"I want you to do me a little favor. Kidnap the president of the United States."

Jake brushed the spiders off him; it was like batting away metal ornaments. "Why would I do that?"

Chromosome shrugged. "Why not? In return I will give you . . . *Psych*."

Jake's eyes narrowed. "How do you know I'm looking for him?" He instantly regretted speaking out. Like with Mr. Grimm, his comment had confirmed his intentions.

"Wouldn't everybody seek out the one who snatched *everything* away? I can give you his exact whereabouts, daily routine . . . *give you back your life*. And no matter what that little reptile Chameleon may have told you, the process he used on your family *is* reversible. But only Psych can perform it. Only he possesses that ability. It was one of several powers deemed too dangerous to synthesize."

She folded her arms and raised a perfect eyebrow.

On the Trail

"Do we have a deal?"

Jake gawked. While the task sounded feasible, the ramifications of kidnapping the president were huge. People *would* notice. But being handed Psych would save him so much trouble. Chromosome's intentions were irrelevant to Jake. Once he had his family back he could then turn his attentions on the two warring factions of heroes and villains, and destroy them both.

"We have a deal."

Chromosome looked pleased. "My associate Mr. Grimm will find you at the relevant time and give you the details of the operation. When you hand me the president, I will deliver you to Psych's door."

She headed back up the ramp of the ship, her Legion skittering after her.

"You better not betray me," warned Jake.

Chromosome stopped and whirled around, a look of surprise on her face. "Whatever made you think that?"

"If you don't do *exactly* what you promised, then I will destroy you." Jake hoped that didn't sound like an idle threat.

Chromosome's surprised expression turned back into her winning smile. "They were right about you. Smart. How fast you boys grow up."

Then she left, the Council shuttle silently taking off, heading back the way it had come. Jake momentarily thought about following, but decided against it.

Although he didn't like it, Jake just had to wait and see how things would turn out.

Lorna had been true to her word and was waiting for Jake as he cautiously approached her house. Once they were safely in the garage, he noticed that she looked immensely tired, but she shook off any questions by saying that she'd had a hectic day.

She had laid out a camping air mattress with several thick blankets and provided Jake with a clean set of clothes that she'd sneaked out of her brother's closet. She had also prepared a chicken and rice frozen meal in the microwave, and there was juice to drink. To Jake it felt like paradise.

Lorna watched him with concern as he ate, and he deflected her questions about the arguments with his family by simply saying he didn't want to talk about it. Instead they talked about movies they had seen recently, music, what they both didn't like about school—although Jake's list was much longer than Lorna's—sports, and anything else they could think about.

Jake was used to talking to his sister, but talking to Lorna was a whole new experience. She was smart, but not in a way that made him feel stupid, and she was much funnier than his old gang. It wasn't as though he was talking to a *girl* at all.

On the Trail

* * *

It was difficult to sleep. While thoughts of revenge powered his every step, the moment Jake sat down and had time to think, Chromosome's ambitious plan to kidnap the president weighed on his mind. He had kidnapped before, a flabby Ukrainian businessman who wasn't expecting to be snatched away by a supervillain. But the president was a different matter. He would be seriously protected. At the time Jake didn't care why Chromosome wanted him to do it, but now the enormity of the task was making him wonder if the risks were worth it.

He shook the doubts away. Of course the risks were worth it. It was for his family.

No, he corrected himself, *I'm doing it for me.*

The following morning Jake and Lorna left her house very early before the rest of her family woke up. They decided to catch a train to a Six Flags theme park in the next town. Jake had asked for sunscreen to protect his skin. Since overdosing on the Villain.net powers he had become pale and sensitive to bright light. Even a cold winter sky could make his skin smart. He also asked for a cap. Lorna gave him her New York Yankees baseball cap, which he pulled low over his face. But he need not have worried as nobody took any notice of him.

The park was packed despite the cold, overcast day, but at least it wasn't raining and people were enjoying the Christmas parades and jovial atmosphere. Lorna had paid for them both to get in, and bought hot dogs to eat in between multiple rides on roller coasters that had them screaming all the way—although Jake had to pretend he was scared as the experience was *nothing* compared to what he'd done over the last few weeks. But the rides and Lorna's company prevented him from dwelling on the enormous task Chromosome had given him. He was determined to enjoy the moment and not think about the future. At least for today.

As they sat enjoying a Coke, he noticed that Lorna seemed thoughtful.

"What's the matter?"

"I was just thinking that you're much nicer than people think."

Jake remained silent. If only he could tell her the truth.

Lorna continued, refusing to meet his gaze. "I mean, you're fun. And not a total idiot."

"Thanks," Jake said, trying to decipher if that was a compliment or not.

"So I was wondering if this . . . you know, made us boyfriend-girlfriend?"

She looked embarrassed and Jake had to look away as he felt suddenly confused.

"Well, um . . . I . . . "

On the Trail

He closed his eyes; he was stammering like a fool. He took a deep breath and turned to Lorna. She was smiling, amused by his unease. Her hand snaked across the table and gently touched his.

Jake's eyes went wide and he suddenly shouted at the top of his lungs.

"Oh my God!"

Lorna snapped her hand back, frightened and confused by his reaction. It took a second for her to realize that Jake was looking over her shoulder. She turned to see the massive figure of Teratoid smash through several snack kiosks, roaring like a gorilla as it batted away two orange-coated security guards.

Jake immediately knew the creature was after him. He grabbed Lorna's hand.

"Listen to me. I . . . I'm going to call the police. Meet me at the gate!"

Lorna nodded. It didn't occur to her to point out that Jake had a cell phone and could have called from anywhere as they both ran.

Screams rippled through the crowds, and Jake found himself pushing against the crush of people trying to flee. He leaped over the counter of a shooting range stall to avoid the crowd. He couldn't just face this foe in public, he'd be recognized instantly—and Lorna would know his secret. But luck was with Jake: a motorcycle helmet and a worn leather jacket lay behind the counter, left by an employee eager to save his skin. Jake put on the helmet, and pulled down the tinted visor. With the jacket it was a perfect disguise.

Jake soared into the air and unleashed a fireball at the monster below. The beast howled in rage and searched the skies to locate its attacker. That's when Jake saw Teratoid's face.

"Scuffer?" he said in astonishment.

Scuffer snarled. He recognized that the voice belonged to a mortal enemy. But the voice woke a painful memory. Now Scuffer didn't see Jake as somebody he had to locate—he saw him as someone he had to *destroy*.

Flexing his mighty muscles, Scuffer leaped toward Jake—easily making a thirty-foot jump from a standing start. Scuffer slammed into Jake midair and they both fell back to earth, smashing through the wooden spars of an old roller coaster like demolition balls.

Jake rolled across the ground as they landed, splashing through one of the stagnant ponds that decorated the ride's grounds. Scuffer was already on his feet and snarling with rage.

"Scuff, what the hell happened to you?"

Scuffer launched himself at Jake, smashing into him with a rugby tackle. Jake was winded and sure some of his bones had cracked. He was lucky, they would repair themselves in a few seconds' time, but he still felt the pain.

On the Trail

They crashed into a steel support pole and the entire roller coaster rattled. A punch from Scuffer landed in his stomach so hard that he was lifted off his feet and flew two hundred feet through a variety of brick and plasterboard walls before hitting the raised pneumatic arm of a spinning Enterprise wheel—the ride was already at top speed, gravity pinning the riders to the wall of the cage fifteen yards above the ground. Jake ricocheted from the ride and crunched through the railing of the park and across a busy road. Cars honked their horns and skidded to avoid him. His head felt groggy, but he looked up as the sound of tearing metal caught his attention.

The entire Enterprise wheel was revolving with such force it wrenched itself from the damaged arm. Full of screaming people, the circular cage shot through the air like a Frisbee.

Lorna had been hiding around the side of the bumper cars, watching as the motorcycle-helmeted hero fought the brute. She wondered who the hero was and felt a stab of jealousy that he was taking the limelight. Lorna was a superhero too. Together with her brother and two friends, they had stumbled across Hero.com and had been downloading superpowers—until it had suddenly malfunctioned two days ago.

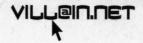
Typical, she thought. The moment for her to shine and actually act like a hero in the public eye was being snatched away because, with Hero.com off-line, her powers were unreliable. She should be saving the day and claiming the fame—something she had desired for so long.

Lorna flexed her arms. Though the powers were glitchy, she had *some* powers stored in her body after the Web site had exploded right in front of her. She looked up in time to see the creature smash the new hero through the roller-coaster stanchions.

She spotted a cart that offered monster masks as prizes and slipped on a rubber witch disguise. Lorna had trouble seeing through the narrow eye slits, and when she finally turned back to the action the hero was bouncing off the Enterprise wheel. The entire structure started to wobble, fragments of metal spinning off the gimbal arm—then the wheel tore itself free and shot through the sky toward her.

Lorna flung herself skyward—and fell flat on her face. The power of flight she thought she possessed had chosen that moment to vanish.

Jake saw that the wheel was going to land on an ugly witchlike figure picking herself up off the ground. The witch suddenly blew jets of ice from its hands. The ice rapidly formed between the ground and the wheel, plucking it from the air.

The disk's momentum was too great for the ice to hold it, and several frozen columns shattered like glass before the wheel abruptly halted less than two feet from crushing the hero. People inside the wheel were flung against the cage walls, breaking bones and smashing noses—but at least they were alive.

A loud horn got Jake's attention and he looked sidelong to see a bus feet away from crushing his head. . . .

WHAM! Scuffer bolted from the theme park and straight into the road, intent on getting Jake. Instead he got ten tons of bus in his back.

Jake flew upward like a jack-in-the-box and watched as the front of the bus buckled around Scuffer's broad shoulders. They skidded together across the road, Scuffer's feet gouging troughs in the tarmac.

Jake readied another fireball and blasted Scuffer. The front of the bus caught fire; the injured driver and his terrified passengers bailed out of emergency exits. Scuffer howled in pain as his hair caught fire, but rather than douse the flames he lashed out.

Lorna watched in astonishment as the mysterious helmeted superhero just about dodged a car the brute hurled at him. She glanced at her impromptu ice claw; it creaked ominously but seemed to be supporting the wheel.

Jake ducked as the unrelenting Scuffer threw more cars at him. The brute ran forward, effortlessly scooping up the vehicles. Not all of the cars were empty either; Jake had a fleeting glimpse of drivers and passengers screaming as they hurtled past, landing on top of other vehicles to form a massive pileup.

Jake had had enough. He felt his anger rise, and his body glowed green as the radioactive power he had mastered formed in his hands. The blast was powerful. Scuffer was pushed onto his back and surfed several yards down the street, crashing headfirst into the mangled bus.

Lorna ran through the hole in the fence and watched as the brute was thrown back into the bus. This close she could see its deformed face and she was reminded of the ugly kid who used to be Jake's pal at school. She raised her hands and fired what she *hoped* was a fireball.

Jake watched as the witch unleashed a spray of water from her hands. It had the intensity of a fire hose, but did little to faze Scuffer. The witch stared at her hands as though she hadn't expected that to happen. She was

On the Trail

too distracted to see Scuffer lift the end of the bus and swing it around like a baseball bat—right at her.

Lorna looked up in time to see the massive bulk of twisted bus arc toward her. She raised her hands in a futile display of self-defense and looked to the helmeted hero.

"Help!"

Jake heard the plea and sneered, "Tough luck!" The visor hid his expression. The bus slammed into the witch with a hollow clang, sending her flying through the air like a struck baseball.

One lousy hero less, thought Jake.

WHAM! Jake didn't see Scuffer swing the bus back. But he felt it connect with his body. He saw his shimmering shield take most of the impact before his vision was swamped with stars—and he was pitched back into the theme park.

Pain racked his body as he soared through the air and struck a steel drop tower—the kind of ride that shot people straight into the air before they plummeted back to earth in a free fall. Jake hit the tower and crumpled back to the ground with such force the concrete around him cracked, as did the motorcycle helmet.

Scuffer bellowed and charged at Jake.

"Oh boy!" Jake murmured, and raised his hands to fire at the seemingly indestructible mutant.

Scuffer suddenly stopped in his tracks and gripped

his throat. He bellowed, clutching at the collar around his neck before he toppled over, unconscious. Jake stared at his hands. What had he done?

A long black Chinook helicopter thundered over the park, the tail ramp open and several armed Enforcers hanging from the back. The chopper landed at the side of the road, the rotor wash causing some of the stacked cars behind it to topple off one another.

Some Enforcers surrounded Scuffer. Two more ran to where Jake had been lying moments earlier.

"The kid's gone!" an Enforcer shouted before they ran back to the chopper.

Across the park, Lorna yanked off her mask. She was drenched in sweat and thankful that her shield power had decided to activate at the crucial moment the bus struck. That's what had saved her. She pushed through the crowds that had formed to watch the fight and ran for the entrance gate.

Jake was already there. She ran toward him and hugged him.

"That was horrible!" she said.

"I saw."

Jake gritted his teeth as she squeezed him tightly; not all his bones had knitted back together yet. He pulled the cap over his eyes and guided Lorna away from the carnage as Scuffer was hoisted under the Chinook and it lifted off. Already the Enforcers were grouping witnesses together. Lorna was curious as to what excuse they could possibly spin to keep this story out of the press.

Jake's mind was a jumble of thoughts. The witch had proved that there were some part-time heroes still out there. And the revelation that Scuffer was still alive had surprised him. Jake felt no compassion for what his ex-friend had become. In fact, it alleviated some of the guilt he had been feeling since he thought he'd killed Scuffer. At least the traitor got what he deserved, although Jake hoped they wouldn't cross paths again. That was the first time he had suffered such a severe beating, and it wasn't pleasant.

He was just glad Lorna had been smart enough to keep out of the way. At least she was a friend he could rely on to treat him like a normal person.

That's just what he needed right now. Someone *normal* he could trust.

A New Home

Chameleon stood in a spacious aircraft hangar. On a normal day, it would be filled with Enforcer helicopters, but at the moment it only had one Chinook from which an unconscious Teratoid was being lifted and strapped back into his reinforced clamps. Reports of Enforcer losses were coming in heavy and fast since the fall of Hero.com. The United Nations had made a valiant effort to suppress the truth, but blaming the rising troubles across the globe on terrorists was becoming harder to swallow.

Now Teratoid had destroyed a theme park in what seemed like a false trail to Hunter. After all, why would an international fugitive take time out to sit on a few rides? The government's spin doctors were hard at work trying to explain that a wild elephant had rampaged through the theme park. Normally they would use Psych to help cover up such a story, but the Prime was in hiding. Now they only had low-level mind control available.

Chameleon was having a moment of doubt that felt

dark and ominous. He'd always believed in doing the right thing, following the unwritten code of the hero. But now, just when the world was sinking into oblivion because the balance between good and evil had been upset—upset with the smallest of viruses—ninety-nine percent of the Primes had run to the hills. Maybe he should run too?

The Foundation headquarters had been repositioned somewhere in the Gobi desert, and their leader, Eric Kirby, had been instructing Chameleon, and the few Primes left fighting the futile battle, to stop the Council of Evil's coordinated attacks. With the few Primes busy trying to protect the world's population, the fate of the Hero Foundation rested on four rookie superheroes, the only Downloaders who, by chance, had been taking powers from Hero.com when it crashed. They were the only heroes available to prevent Basilisk and his team of evildoers from toppling the Hero Foundation.

Back at Diablo Island, Chameleon and several Foundation scientists had calculated that Hunter's ability to store powers and then amplify them to a much more potent level could be used to *replace* the entire Hero network, and the V-net system too. Couple that with his latent power to *create* previously unseen powers, and the potential was earth-shattering. Although the Foundation had long ago learned how to recreate the powers that heroes had willingly donated (and villains forcibly donated), they had never been able to "mix and match" to create new ones. The effects during trials had always been lethal.

Chameleon knew that since he had let Jake slip through his fingers on Diablo Island, Kirby was punishing him by demanding that *he* get Hunter back.

The boy had become the ultimate weapon for both the heroes *and* the villains. Whichever side he was on, it would be the winning one. Hunter's abilities made him a truly frightening opponent.

Chameleon left the hangar and descended to the private underground railway station. There he took a small bullet train for some twenty miles to the Foundation hospital.

The moment he left the train and entered the subterranean command center, he was assaulted by Enforcer staff all demanding his attention. Huge screens on the wall depicted the planet, airspace above, and even sections of the moon. Different colored graphics showed the deployment of Enforcer, Council, or Foundation forces—and Chameleon didn't need to look to see who was winning. The glow from the screen made the entire command center look as if they were on red alert.

"One at a time," said Chameleon, taking his seat behind the controller's desk. He hated this administrative part of his job; he would much rather be out in the field, fighting. Actually, he would much rather be sitting in bed with a hot chocolate and watching repeats of *The Simpsons* because his body ached from the constant punishment it had taken recently.

A nerdy-looking Enforcer technician thrust a tablet PC at him. "Sir, while you've been away the kids, uh, I mean, Toby Wilkinson's team, lost Basilisk—"

"What?" Chameleon was on his feet again. "I thought we had Enforcer patrols bringing him in?"

"They were too late. Long story." He looked at the notes on his computer tablet and ticked them off like a shopping list. "Loss of assets, multiple witnesses, Pete kidnapped, Mexico lead, blah, blah."

Chameleon looked at him in astonishment. "What? Don't 'blah-blah' me! Tell me everything."

"It's all in the report. Without you here, Mr. Grimm acted on it right away."

Chameleon sat back down. He never felt comfortable when Grimm's name was mentioned, but for some reason Eric Kirby trusted him. And Eric was the boss. Chameleon thought, for the good of his blood pressure, he'd read the report later.

Another techie offered a similar tablet PC, but snatched it back when he saw the look on Chameleon's face.

"Just *read it* to me," said Chameleon, rubbing his eyes.

"Government demands to know why Teratoid

demolished a theme park and injured thirty-eight people. And they have demanded more Enforcer units to guard the capital."

"As long as you don't tell them it was a mistake, make something up. Run some static and say Teratoid escaped or something."

"Oh. So it wasn't a mistake?"

Chameleon stared at the techie. The man glanced at his colleagues, none of whom offered any support. They were all nervous from working so close to a Super.

"We examined security cameras of the park and used facial recognition software to—"

"Just show me," sighed Chameleon, leaning forward on his desk.

The techie used his tablet computer to change one of the large display screens to show various security footage of the park prior to Scuffer's attack. A square icon scanned the faces of the crowd. Sections of face—an eye here, an ear there—rapidly changed on-screen. It was like watching a police photo lineup done as a flip book. Soon Jake Hunter's face appeared, and the computer flashed the words "POSITIVE MATCH." Despite concealing his face under the cap, the computer had still managed to take information from the structure of Jake's face, in the same way a biometric passport photo did.

Chameleon couldn't take his eyes from the screen. "My God, he really did show up. Why?"

"Not sure, sir. There was no reported sighting of Chromosome in the area."

"Who's the girl with him?"

The techie isolated images of Jake's companion, and Chameleon felt a knot of worry in his stomach as he recognized her immediately.

"Lorna!" Chameleon nervously drummed his fingers on the desk. She was a hero—what was she doing with Hunter? Was she aware of the situation she'd placed herself in? "Get me Grimm on the phone. Where is Toby Wilkinson's team now?"

The maps on the screen highlighted a blue dot.

"They've just left on an Aurora Stealth Bomber, heading for Mexico. They're running radio silence," reported a female technician. "Lorna's with them and Grimm isn't responding to his phone."

"Okay, don't bother with Grimm. I'll handle this. Open up all surveillance circuits and find me Hunter!"

Chameleon slumped back, more exhausted than ever. There was nothing more he could do right now and he needed to sleep or he'd be of no use to anybody. He didn't know why Lorna was with Hunter, but it didn't bode well.

He closed his eyes; if he knew Hunter, he was sure to surface on the criminal radar very soon.

* * *

It was late afternoon when Jake and Lorna had returned home. He had been afraid that she would bring up the afternoon's events, but luckily she didn't. Nobody was at her house and Jake retrieved his laptop. There was an awkward moment when they said good-bye and exchanged cell numbers; Lorna told him not to call until later tonight, as a friend had borrowed her phone.

Jake walked away and felt a tremor of elation. Apart from the attacking mutated ex-friend and destruction of the theme park, it had been a great day.

His phone vibrated in his pocket. It was a text message from Mr. Grimm asking to meet. Jake sighed. He couldn't help but feel that he was being used again, but he desperately needed a lead to Psych. Jake thought over the situation. He always seemed to be at a disadvantage because he was relying on other people. He knew from school-yard warfare that the only way out of such a bitter cycle was to change the rules. He was trading the president for information; how could he switch that around and place himself in a superior position to Chromosome?

That was something to think about.

The meeting wasn't for another couple of hours, so Jake took a risk and visited his family again. They were at home, and Jake didn't want to enter the house while they were inside. Last time he'd done that, Enforcers had stormed the place. From across the street, Jake

could see small dome-shaped sensors in the front garden, telltale signs that they were under surveillance,
but luckily it seemed the Enforcers were stretched too
thin to spare the manpower to have an actual agent
keep an eye on them.

Jake satisfied himself by sitting on the wall of the
house across the street and trying to look through the
window. He could see his parents talking and Jake provided his own soundtrack.

"I wonder where our son is? You mean Jake? Isn't he a
great boy . . . " Jake shut up, feeling embarrassed that
he'd even put on a silly high-pitched voice to narrate. He
suddenly felt an overwhelming sense of loss, and wished
he could just walk across the street, ring the bell, and be
greeted by warm hugs and welcoming faces.

An elderly neighbor, Mrs. Bowen, passed Jake with a
bunch of shopping bags. She was a friend of the family
but she didn't cast a single glance at Jake, and he wondered if Psych had wiped the memories of his entire
family and their friends? If so, why not the people at
school? Lorna still recognized him. And Knuckles and
Big Tony certainly did.

Jake turned away from his old home; being here was
not doing him any good. He vowed to himself that he'd
only return once he had the means to unlock their
minds and they could be a family once more. He took a
few steps, then hesitated. Loud music was drifting from

Beth's bedroom. He strained to listen, and could hear his dad's voice.

"Bethany, turn down that music!"

Despite his sadness, Jake couldn't help but smile. He recognized the music as something Beth would ordinarily hate, but for some reason she was playing it loud. It was Jake's favorite band, Ironfist.

Somewhere in Beth's head were rebellious threads of memory about her brother. And that gave Jake a sudden flush of confidence.

Mr. Grimm was never ever late. Punctuality was a sign of character. It defined a person's integrity and reliability. In Mr. Grimm's opinion it was more important than honesty and loyalty. Loyalty was just a matter of opinion; punctuality was a matter of breeding.

Jake was twenty-three minutes late, which was an achievement, since he had nothing to do except while away the hours. He'd done that by leaving a few text messages on Lorna's cell, then stopped because he didn't want to look too interested.

Before leaving for his meeting, Jake went to his father's shed to hide the laptop. He was trembling slightly, a sign he needed to replenish his power. He connected the laptop to the cell phone and accessed Villain.net. The site was pretty much the same. He clicked on the flashing news banner and read through a page depicting the Council of Evil's progress in what they described as *"a war."*

Jake refreshed his powers with a few random selections. Rejuvenated, he noticed the "LOW BATTERY" icon was flashing in the corner of the screen. Seconds later the laptop suddenly turned itself off. Jake hesitated. The only power sockets were in the house, along with Beth's power pack to charge it. He decided to leave it for now, but a quick glance at the cell phone revealed that its battery level was also in the red zone. And he didn't have a charger for that.

Jake panicked. His only two access points to Villain.net were running flat. Without constant access to powers to feed his addiction, he would die!

Jake took a deep breath, trying to calm his nerves. His latest fix would keep him going for several hours. He would have to arrange something else after he met Grimm.

Not showing any signs of feeling the chill wind that blew across the top floor of the multilevel parking lot, Mr. Grimm repressed every urge to rebuke Jake for his tardiness. Instead he tried to smile, but managed nothing more than a grimace.

"Mr. Hunter, I'm so glad you turned up." The unspoken word "finally" hung in the air.

"You have some info?"

"I have so much more than *that* for you. Please, come with me."

Mr. Grimm gestured across the empty parking lot. Jake frowned.

"Where to?"

"To your new home, if you'll have it."

Jake followed Grimm's hand, and this time noticed the air next to him was wavering slightly, as though it were liquefied. Jake instantly sensed a trap. Mr. Grimm must have picked up on his thoughts.

"Please, follow me."

Mr. Grimm sidestepped into the portal and vanished. Jake hesitated—then reacted as Mr. Grimm's head poked back from the portal although the rest of his body was unseen. It was like talking to a severed head.

"Quickly now."

Jake tensed himself, ready for anything, then followed Grimm through the shimmering portal. He stepped out into a large stone-flagged hall, close to a roaring fireplace that was taller than he was.

"Where are we?"

"Romania. Follow me."

Mr. Grimm opened a door and Jake followed him down a stone corridor that was lit by recessed lights. The walls were large bricks, and their footsteps echoed spookily. It felt as if they were in an old castle that somebody had tried to modernize. Grimm climbed up

A New Home

a large spiraling staircase that went on for some time. Eventually they entered a spacious circular room that was bare except for two massive plasma screens sitting side by side on stands, the images on them fed from several computers. Jake instantly recognized Villain.net on one and a twenty-four-hour news channel on the other.

Then he noticed a balcony area beyond a set of double glazed doors that swished open as Mr. Grimm approached. They stepped out into the icy cold. Mr. Grimm gestured around him.

"Your new home."

They were standing at the top of a single spire that gave them a view of the castle below. Jake had guessed correctly; it was an old castle built on the edge of a cliff top that dropped into blackness below. The castle itself wasn't huge, but it was more than big enough for Jake. Around them sat jagged snow-covered mountains, the peaks of many smothered by thick clouds.

"The Transylvanian Alps; they're part of the southern Carpathian Mountains," said Mr. Grimm in his monotone voice that was oddly fitting in this setting. He looked at Jake as though that should mean something, but Jake was drawing a blank. "The legendary home of Dracula?"

"Oh," said Jake, feeling more than a little creeped out.

"The landscape was inspiration for Bram Stoker's

character. And a fitting lair for a supervillain, don't you think?"

"I don't get it. Chromosome is giving me this?"

Mr. Grimm shook his head and looked out across the vista. "No. I am. I'm not an employee of the Council. I just work for them as a contractor. In fact I work for a great many people, including the Hero Foundation. But the views of my employers never interfere with my work . . . except in this one instance. I have been following your progress with great interest, Mr. Hunter. You're stuck in the middle of a war."

"Like Switzerland," said Jake, remembering some of the history lessons about World War Two. That and the dinosaurs were definitely the best parts of history.

"No. Switzerland was neutral, and not under threat from opposing sides. You are something else." Jake frowned, but decided not to question him. "I'm unsure what Chromosome's full plans for you are. My employers only tell me what *they think* I need to know. I do know she thinks that by controlling the president she can control the largest military might on the planet."

"Who would she attack? The Council? The Foundation?"

"*Everybody*. You must learn that when you swim on your own, the sharks will eat you." Mr. Grimm looked back at Jake, his face pale and calculating. "Unless you are swimming with the shark with the biggest bite. Like me."

Jake's head began to spin with animal metaphors. He hated this kind of thing. Basilisk was always secretive and had spoken in riddles, claiming that Jake was just a kid who wouldn't understand. But now Grimm was speaking as though Jake understood the cryptic references. As much as he loathed admitting it, Basilisk had a point; he was just a kid who was frightened and confused. But that was a weakness he knew he couldn't show.

"So all this is yours, and you are offering it to me? Why? What's in it for you?"

"Balance. I am not interested in exploiting you, Mr. Hunter. Sure, you can use your powers and rule the world, gathering riches from across continents. But then I would inevitably be working for *you*. No, that's not what I want. I require that you do . . . whatever it is you wish to. You desire to get your family back, fine. You want to try and bring down the Foundation or the Council; that is fine too. As long as there is a balance between the two forces, I can do what I do, and reap the rewards."

"So you're just a mercenary?"

"A mercenary who respects that no one side should be all-powerful. I must look out for myself, after all."

That made perfect sense to Jake. It seemed that he and the enigmatic Mr. Grimm held very similar views. Jake wondered if he'd found an ally.

Mr. Grimm continued. "Right now the Hero Foundation is suffering, which somewhat upsets things. But plans are afoot to stabilize this. I do not wish to live in a world dominated by the Council. That would be most . . . boring."

"How does Chromosome fit into all this?"

Mr. Grimm shrugged his bony shoulders. "You and she have a deal. I suggest that you honor it as best you can. She does not know about this lair, and you should keep it that way in case she tries to double-cross you. Not that I have any evidence that she will. Still, you need to be prepared."

Jake shivered as he started to feel the cold. He was being given a place to call his own, and some advice from a man who was also offering friendship. Or, at the very least, Grimm was somebody who didn't openly seem to want to use him.

He looked around the castle. Not so long ago all this had seemed so important. He had dreamed of riches and his own place—preferably on the warm beaches of Australia rather than the freezing peaks of the Carpathian Mountains. But those dreams now seemed immaterial. He realized that he wasn't chasing new riches—he was simply trying to retrieve what he had taken for granted and lost.

"So you're not going to tell me what to do, or expect me to rob a bank for you or something?"

A New Home

"My goals are completely selfish. They are to strike a balance between the Foundation and the Council. Both empires are too shortsighted to bother looking into the future. If they did take the time, they would see a potential threat is waiting, preparing to wipe us *all* out."

Jake was expecting a lecture on the destruction of the environment, but when he caught Mr. Grimm's expression he realized that it was something worse, and much more imminent.

"What would they see?"

Grimm's face flickered for a moment, and Jake saw a glimmer of hopelessness before it was masked again.

"The end of the world."

Jake's mouth opened but nothing came out. Could there be problems much bigger than the ones he was facing now? The end of the world did seem like a pretty severe outcome.

Grimm spun on his heels and entered the tower. "Come. I have instructions from Chromosome that you must see."

Jake followed, casting one last glance at his new mountaintop home. With a bit of work he might actually get to like it here.

Chameleon was woken from sleep by the door buzzer. He looked around his cramped dormitory to get his bearings. The Foundation provided accommodation in all its outposts, but the command center under the hospital was not built for comfort.

He climbed from bed and opened the door, which swung on creaky hinges. They were also not very generous with the technology used in the private quarters. Would it have killed them to install automatic sliding doors?

Chameleon stared at the command center supervisor in front of him.

"Sorry to disturb you, sir, but you wanted to know if Mr. Grimm showed up?"

Before going to bed, Chameleon had spoken to the command center supervisor and asked him to monitor Grimm's movements. He had to keep it quiet as Grimm was a favorite of the boss, and it wasn't good business to spy on your colleagues. But since Grimm had apparently abandoned Toby, Pete, Lorna, and Emily—the only group of heroic Downloaders left— while on a mission to Diablo Island, Chameleon had grown suspicious. And the link between Lorna and Jake made his stomach churn. He couldn't put his finger on it, but something about Grimm just didn't feel right. He hoped it was a case of unfounded paranoia.

"Well?"

"He spent some time waiting on top of a multilevel parking lot alone."

A New Home

"Who met him?"

"We don't know. We would not have known he was there if our spy satellites hadn't picked up on an energy signature specific to his portal generation skills. Then he vanished."

"Do you know where to?"

The man shook his head. Chameleon was annoyed with the news.

"Don't tell anybody about this. Let me investigate. I'll be out of communication for a while."

Chameleon shut the door and looked thoughtfully around. He only needed a few hours' sleep to feel in tip-top condition. It wasn't a superpower, it was just his natural rhythm. He quickly changed clothes as he thought about his strategy.

Though just schoolkids, Toby, Lorna, Emily, and Pete were important assets to the Foundation. Chameleon had become fond of them, although he always maintained a professional demeanor in his rare talks with Toby. He would much rather be out helping Toby's team, but instead he was tasked with finding Hunter, the thorn in his side. If Toby's team failed in their mission, then the Hero Foundation would fall.

He cursed himself for not fighting harder to ensure that Mr. Grimm didn't oversee Toby's team. He couldn't allow any harm to come to them—but he also couldn't allow Jake Hunter to walk free and risk capture

by the Council. By finding Hunter, Chameleon could stop Hunter's friendship with Lorna from developing any further and potentially getting out of hand. And hopefully he'd discover if his suspicions about Mr. Grimm had any grains of truth.

The last thing the Foundation needed was a spy in its ranks.

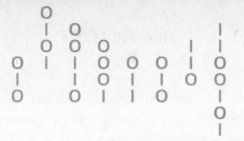

Air Force One

Mr. Grimm had disappeared on urgent business, leaving Jake several hours to explore his new home. It was bigger than he'd thought. Almost every room had a television and a computer. He discovered an enormous kitchen that was equipped to feed an army, and luckily had a microwave in the corner. He could use it to nuke one of the many meals stashed in the walk-in freezer.

Jake decided he needed a few diabolical plans of his own so that he could afford a catering staff and a butler. Already his mental tally of finances was adding up, and he understood why Basilisk was always complaining that he was broke. Evil lairs were expensive places to run. He wondered if he'd be expected to pay bills.

The castle extended down, via one long staircase, to an underground hangar. It was empty and Jake imagined filling it up with all kinds of expensive toys.

He felt a little lonely in the vast castle and, in an effort to keep his thoughts off his family, found that he was thinking about Lorna. She was fun, and he enjoyed being with her even if their first date had turned into a wrestling match with a mutant.

He'd like to see her again. That was a strange enough thought. Snooping around earlier, he'd found an adapter that fitted his phone. When it was fully recharged, he tried calling Lorna, but the phone just rang until it went to voice mail. He hung up, suddenly feeling stupid for calling. Perhaps he should wait for *her* to call first? But if *he* waited then maybe *she* would think . . .

He shook his head. Bringing Lorna into the equation made things more complicated. Instead he tasked himself with finally getting the second enormous television working and channel-surfed through hours of reruns. He stopped at a news channel that was showing live reports from around the world. Everywhere there seemed to be fighting, looting, and explosions. It was utter chaos. The newscasters talked of troublemakers provoking crowds, organized criminals taking advantage of overstretched security, and terrorists coordinating attacks. But Jake knew it was the work of overzealous supervillains.

Mr. Grimm finally appeared through a portal, so silently that he startled Jake. Grimm did not waste any further time as he explained Chromosome's plan to kidnap the president.

It was ambitious. In many ways it was the biggest task Jake had ever faced. Literally.

Chromosome didn't just want the president; she wanted him *and* Air Force One—the president's private aircraft. Chromosome had designed the plan to cause maximum shock and awe to the population. Of course that made Jake's task all the more difficult.

"I still don't know *who* Chromosome is. Why should I trust a member of the Council?"

Grimm looked at his watch before deciding to speak. "You know what the Council is. Chromosome has one of the eight seats of power and has ambitions to run the Council herself. And she could. She is manipulative, ruthless, and has a skill to create life from inanimate objects. She calls them her Legion. You have seen them in the form of the metal spiders that follow her everywhere. Be careful of them; they are not what they seem. Chromosome does indeed have the power to help you. But she also has her own agenda."

A snort of mirthless laughter escaped Jake. He wasn't surprised; everybody had their own agendas. It probably explained why *nobody* ever succeeded in ruling the world—too many conflicts of interest. "And what is her agenda exactly?"

"She has been sowing the seeds of uprising within the Council. The job of heading the Council is supposed to rotate among members. But for some time it has stayed with the one they call Necros. And he has built up supporters from within the Council's own

ranks. Chromosome sees the logical outcome being that eventually Necros will declare himself as supreme leader and will have no need for the other Council members."

"So she'll bump him off and run the show?"

"Colorfully put. And if she has the president under her control, then she has the world's most powerful army at her disposal *and* the Council of Evil at her fingertips. It's not a difficult equation to work out."

Mr. Grimm selected the powers that Jake was likely to need for his mission from Villain.net and stepped to the other side of the room as the snaking probe extended from the screen. For a moment it seemed as though the probe would seek out Grimm, but after wavering, it swung toward Jake.

Now Jake felt fully energized—better than ever, in fact. He suspected that Grimm had inserted a few extra powers to rev him up. Once Grimm was satisfied that Jake knew what he was doing, he excused himself and slipped through a portal without wishing Jake good luck.

Jake opened his eyes again as he flew through cotton-ball-like cumulonimbus clouds. His flying power was more potent than the first one he'd tried—Mr. Grimm had explained that there were several "strengths" of powers available. Jake could now breathe easily at high altitudes, and he didn't feel the ice-cold winds as he had when he escaped the island prison.

He glanced at the GPS strapped to his wrist. It had been one of the gadgets in his tower. Grimm had explained how to set the global positioning satellite coordinates. It had also been programmed with his target's predicted destination, which was tricky because the target was moving.

At least it was daylight and the weather around him was good. He had relatively clear views across the North Atlantic Ocean, which was dotted with white chunks of ice. His GPS told him he was right on target, a couple of hundred miles off the Canadian coast. Now he would have to rely on observation to locate what he was seeking.

It took several minutes before he saw the glint of sunlight on the white paint of an aircraft. He estimated it was about two miles away. Jake kicked out, gaining a little extra height as he circled around the back of his target.

As he drew near, the writing along the fuselage became clearer. The words "UNITED STATES OF AMERICA" ran along the center of the aircraft in bold letters. Underneath the writing a sky-blue strip ran the length of the Boeing VC-25A, a military version of the 747, before it spread across the front cockpit. The Stars and Stripes were painted on the tail, over the flight number "29000."

This was the one Jake wanted, his target: Air Force One.

Two F-22 Raptor fighters escorted the aircraft. When the threat from the failure of Hero.com spread to major cities, the president had taken to the air to monitor the crisis from there. The vice president had been bundled aboard a similar aircraft, designated Air Force Two, which was circling the opposite ocean—the Pacific.

Jake flew closer and focused on the task at hand. This was a daring stunt. He reminded himself that he was doing this solely to get the information to win back his family, and surely that should override any doubts he had.

But it didn't. No matter how much Jake weighed it, what he was about to do was nothing short of an act of war. And once he handed the president over to Chromosome . . . he tried to ignore those thoughts. That wasn't his problem. *Shouldn't* be his problem . . .

"Get a grip," he murmured to himself.

The fighter escort and crew of Air Force One would have no idea he was trailing them; he was too small to show up on radar. On board Air Force One there were fifty people. Aside from crew, there would be the president, secretary of defense, military aides, and five-star generals as well as Secret Service bodyguards who were trained to jump in the path of bullets to protect the president.

Grimm had told him to kill any nonessential personnel if they got in his way, but Jake was going to do it *his* way—which consisted mostly of serious improvisation.

He edged closer, angling under the tail wings. From here he could hear the rumble of the four powerful engines pushing the aircraft along at six hundred and thirty miles per hour. His first problem was how to get into a pressurized aircraft without breaking the airtight seal. He had talked with Grimm about downloading teleportation, but teleportation was not accurate enough. Plus there were no photographs of the inside of the craft available, so Jake had no way of correctly visualizing his destination, which was crucial with teleportation.

He was mentally running through his options when he noticed that another aircraft had appeared ahead of them. He squinted, making out a long tube dangling from the back of the new arrival. His first instinct was that it was another plane trying to attack Air Force One, but this proved unfounded when neither F-22 tried to intercept it. As the aircraft grew larger, images from television flooded Jake's mind and he realized what was happening.

It was a huge slate-gray KC-10 refueling plane. It had a hose running out behind it that ended in a drogue, a large shuttlecock-like attachment that slipped over the refueling probes on both fighters and Air Force One. Refueling was a delicate operation that took supreme skill from all pilots involved in the operation. Once connected, jet fuel would refill the aircrafts' tanks, allowing them to stay airborne longer.

Jake felt Air Force One slow down as it positioned itself behind and just under the KC-10. This was a situation Jake hadn't counted on. If he was going to get the president, then he didn't have time to dawdle.

Jake stuck to the fuselage, under the tail section. This allowed him to stop flying and to be carried along like an insect. The wind flow was a lot fiercer here as the air was forced along the fuselage at high speeds. He scuttled along the belly of the craft, so the ground was now above his head. The two escort fighters were positioned just above the Boeing so the pilots could not see him crawl the seventy-five yards toward the nose of the craft.

Where the body of the plane began to taper toward the nose, Jake stopped to get his bearings. He'd tried to memorize the plans Grimm had shown him, but he was still unsure of his exact position. He *should* be directly outside the forward cargo hold. He closed his eyes to make sure he summoned the correct downloaded power; a mistake now could be fatal for both him and for the occupants of the plane.

Air Force One suddenly rocked, making Jake freeze. They must have hit a pocket of air turbulence. Craning his neck, he could see the KC-10 was much closer now, no doubt almost in position. Then he noticed one of the escort fighters had dipped low, forced down by the same turbulence that shook the Boeing. Unfortunately it meant that all that the pilot had to do was turn his head and he would see Jake.

Jake didn't waste any more time. He pushed himself against the solid fuselage—and phased through the metal like a ghost.

Grimm had instructed him on how to use the power. It was all very well phasing into the aircraft—but what lay beyond the wall posed the problem. Jake might re-form halfway through. Grimm had told him a cautionary tale about a supervillain who walked through metal doors to clean out bank vaults. On his last occasion the villain had not known a smaller vault door had been installed beyond the main one—and he had solidified midway through the new door. His heart was suddenly encased in the metal of the new door, resulting in instant death. The authorities found his torso hanging out of the steel door. That's why few people used that power: it was dangerous.

Jake just had to trust to luck that when he made it through there would be no nasty surprises. His vision suddenly turned black, as it had done when he'd made

a few practice phases through the castle walls, but he had a definite sense of movement. Seconds later his head poked through into a cargo area that ran a quarter of the length of the plane and was full of food supply boxes. Jake just about managed to make it through a double stack of boxes before re-forming . . . right in front of a surprised flight attendant, who was pulling a packet of cookies from a supply box. She opened her mouth to scream at the ghost that had just material-ized right in front of her.

Jake gave silent thanks that he hadn't re-formed halfway into the stewardess or they would have both been either killed, or turned into some horrible con-joined twin.

He shot a hand across her mouth to stop the scream, but she bit hard into his fingers. Then she moved with practiced judo precision, levering Jake over her shoul-der in a perfect *seoi nage* throw that slammed him to the floor. He wasn't expecting that. He also wasn't expecting the attendant to reach out and slam a panic button on the wall.

"Great!" snarled Jake; he knew that would bring the Secret Service running. Grimm had warned him that the Secret Service was not to be toyed with, even if he had superpowers. The stewardess spun around to face him again, taking a defensive stance. Jake felt his hands form a small ball of energy, he hoped just enough to knock out the woman. He threw up his hands—and a rain of confetti covered the stewardess. Jake was more stunned than she was. Was this Mr. Grimm's idea of a joke?

"Stupid time for a useless power!"

As he looked up from his hand, he realized that the woman had switched martial arts, and he just saw a blur as her foot crashed into his chest in a perfect karate snap kick. Jake smashed into several boxes, which luckily fell down, blocking the stairwell door just as it was being pushed open by Secret Service personnel.

"I've had enough of this," Jake groaned, surprised to see blood trickling from his nose. It didn't last long before his regeneration stemmed the flow.

The stewardess was ready to pounce again. Jake had to admit that he hadn't expected to be attacked by a kinda pretty flight attendant when he was trying to kidnap the president.

He raised his hand again, this time checking it when he felt a ball of energy form. Sure enough a tennis-ball-size translucent sphere glowed in his palm. He threw it at the girl, where it noisily exploded in kinetic energy and threw her clean through the air. She fell, unconscious.

Jake felt guilty. In all his bullying years he had never hit a girl. Not counting his sister, of course.

The blocked door leading from the cargo area budged as it was rammed from outside. The crates wouldn't hold back the Secret Service guys for long, and when they found the attendant unconscious and alone, they would hopefully assume she had fallen and accidentally hit the alarm.

If Jake's information was correct, then there should be a medical facility directly above his head. He took a flying leap up, phasing through the ceiling just as the Secret Service broke through.

It was an odd experience to phase through the floor, and then suddenly find it solid beneath your feet. But Jake had had a catalog of odd experiences lately, so he didn't give it much thought. He was in what looked like a compact doctor's exam room, with a recliner and an assortment of expensive medical equipment stowed against the wall, including what looked like an X-ray machine. If it hadn't been for the curved wall behind him, Jake would almost have forgotten that he was in an airplane.

A clunking sound reverberated through the aircraft, and the pilot's voice spoke calmly over the PA system.

"Connected for refueling."

That seemed to be all the details Jake was going to get. He took stock of his situation. There was one door leading out into a corridor that ran toward the tail, past the galley and into a large conference room. That meant the wall in front of Jake should be the Presidential Suite, built into the nose of the craft, just under the cockpit. And with any luck, that's where he'd find the president, his primary target. Not that that really mattered, since Chromosome wanted the entire aircraft. As long as the president remained inside it then Jake only had one problem to solve. That was a major challenge for even the most seasoned villain; stealing an aircraft—in-flight—from between its protective fighter escorts. Grimm had told him that an entire aircraft was too big to teleport; otherwise villains would have been teleporting entire bank vaults rather than breaking into them. Instead Chromosome's plan involved Jake persuading the pilot to turn around. If not, the autopilot would do it for him.

Once again Jake had to convince himself it was all worth it. The memory of his sister listening to Ironfist made him smile; there *was* hope for her yet.

The first thing Jake had to do was cut all communications from the aircraft. With over eighty telephones, radios, fax machines, and numerous computer systems it would be easy for anybody aboard the aircraft to make an emergency call. Luckily all calls were routed through a communications room situated behind the cockpit. And that should be just above Jake. He took another flying leap and phased through the ceiling.

After a second of utter blackness as he passed between floors, Jake phased into the room above and immediately knew that his information was incorrect. Tables and luxury, leather-padded revolving chairs, all bolted to the floor, filled his view and he willed himself not to re-form just yet or he would become half boy, half table. He solidified on top of the table, where three very surprised men and one woman stared at him, frozen in terror. It was some kind of planning lounge and Jake found that he was standing amid stacks of papers and maps. Two doors on either end of the room were helpfully labeled "cockpit" and "communications room." A stairwell ran down from this room to the mid-deck.

Jake fired a small energy orb at one of the men, knocking him out of his chair and unconscious to the floor. This bought the woman enough time to dart from her seat and slide—headfirst—down the stairwell. Jake turned to intercept her, but felt something connect with the back of his head and he pitched forward. Luckily this time he had remembered to will his force field around him in case he met any more kung-fu-happy staff. But he still felt the blow and the room spun as he toppled off the table.

He looked up to see that one of the men had pistol-whipped him. Seconds later an alarm squawked through the plane; obviously the woman had raised it. It was enough of a distraction for the two men to look stupidly up at the flickering red light on the ceiling.

Jake let two radioactive streamers rip—punching both men in the stomach and slamming them into the curved bulkhead. They were knocked out, their expensive suits smoldering. Jake had no time for pity—now he was feeling angry that his plan to do this quietly had been sabotaged.

The communications room was a dark place, filled with banks of sophisticated computers lit only by the harsh LCD screens. Four operators didn't have time to look up as the fortified door buckled when it was blown off its hinges. The door struck three of them, taking them out, before it slammed into the expensive hardware in a shower of sparks.

Jake entered looking vengeful. He had planned to deliver a small electromagnetic pulse through the aircraft's communication systems, as Grimm had advised. That would be enough to take them off-line. But now Jake was running on adrenaline, and was doing what came naturally to him—being heavy-handed.

He unleashed a lightning bolt across the room. The crackling electricity struck every system and overloaded them in a fountain of sparks. The last conscious operator in the room couldn't have been more than twenty. He peered at Jake through owl-like glasses.

"Don't shoot!"

"Don't tell me what to do," Jake snarled impulsively. A strand of lightning jumped from his finger and struck the man in the chest. He slumped to the floor in a ball.

Jake ran back into the lounge, which was now lit only by emergency lighting strips—he must have overloaded the ship's electronics. He heard the clatter of feet on the stairs as impeccably dressed Secret Service personnel ran up, armed with automatic pistols. Jake had been told that nobody would risk firing a gun on board, as a bullet hole would depressurize the aircraft. But it looked as if nobody had bothered telling the security services that.

Jake sent another volley of lightning down the stairs. The two leading men, who were so big they barely managed to fit up the staircase, fell backward, cannoning into two more.

Jake ran for the cockpit door, and didn't break his stride as he phased through. The cockpit was jam-packed with flight instrumentation and the windows offered a view of the KC-10 refueling plane right in front of them, with the long fuel pipe trailing out toward the side of the cockpit. Jake could clearly see the shuttlecock drogue connected to the line, just outside the cockpit window. Despite the alarm that was sounding, the crew could not simply stop the refueling process. They were already running on empty tanks.

The pilot didn't even look around as he heard a gasp from the copilot and engineer. He was too busy jiggling the controls to make sure Air Force One remained connected to the refueling pipe.

"I'm going to make this very easy for you," Jake said in a voice that trembled from both nerves and excitement.

"All you have to do is refuel and turn this plane toward Romania. All your radios are out, and in a few minutes you won't have a fighter escort."

"You're hijacking us?"

Jake hesitated. That seemed too strong a word. Then again, telling the pilot that he was kidnapping them all didn't sound any better.

"You'll live. Unless you try something stupid."

"Why are you doing this?" said the terrified copilot, as the cockpit door was repeatedly hammered by Secret Service guys desperate to get in.

"I'm doing this to get my family back. I wish there was another way, but—"

The copilot had been maintaining perfect eye contact, and no flicker gave away the fact that the engineer, who was positioned just to Jake's side, had slid out a high-voltage stun gun. He fired it into Jake's ribs.

Jake felt as though every nerve in his body was on fire as the current pulsed through him. The special-issue stun gun would have felled a bear in seconds—no normal human stood a chance.

But Jake wasn't normal.

The current emerged from his body, amplified. Lightning bolts burst out from him in all directions, striking instruments and crew with such ferocity that Jake could smell burning clothes and hair. Jake himself dropped to the floor, momentarily weakened. When he caught his breath and looked up he saw the entire crew was unconscious and slumped over the controls, even the pilot. Worse still, the instrument panel was dead—lights out, and dials reading zero across the board. He could still hear the engines roaring, so they were still flying, but the sophisticated computer system was dead.

He'd lost the autopilot.

In fact, the roar of the engines seemed *overly* noisy. He stood up and gazed through the cockpit window.

And what he saw was *bad*.

When the pilot had slumped forward, his hand had been on the throttle. It had been pushed by his body weight, and had edged the control to maximum. Air Force One had jolted forward, severing the attached fuel line. Pure aviation fuel splattered across the window like a bad rainstorm.

But that wasn't the worst of it. Air Force One had accelerated so close to the slower KC-10 tanker that the top of the cockpit grated along the tail of the refueling tanker.

The sound of tearing metal reverberated through the Boeing. Jake watched in shock as metal-on-metal sparks kicked up—igniting the volatile jet fuel.

The blue nose of Air Force One erupted in flames as the fuel caught fire. The front of the aircraft was now an orange fireball.

Air Force One

The two F-22 pilots in the opposite planes had never seen anything like it, and they were powerless to help. The KC-10 tanker sharply banked aside—narrowly missing a collision with the Boeing. The trailing fuel hose still spewed liquid fire until automatic cutoff valves stemmed the flow. Air Force One's twisted refueling probe blocked access to the aircraft's fuel tanks, preventing the flames from reaching it and blowing the aircraft up in midair.

Jake dragged the pilot out of his seat as the Boeing climbed sharply. He'd flown flight simulators and even Basilisk's *SkyKar*—but this was a different beast altogether. And there were fifty innocent people on board. He gently pushed the control stick forward and the aircraft leveled out, although all Jake could see through the window was a wall of flames.

With no way to see out, no instruments, and absolutely zero real flying experience sitting behind a jumbo jet, Jake knew he had no choice but to make an emergency landing—otherwise everybody on board would be killed.

Including him.

Splash Down

The F-22 Raptors orbited Air Force One. The entire front was aflame, and the fire threatened to reach the massive wings where the fuel was stored. Then the Boeing began to nose-dive toward the sparkling ocean below. The pilots' repeated attempts to radio the plane met with static. A U.S. naval vessel, the USS *Kitty Hawk*, had already sent rescue helicopters, but they wouldn't arrive for another hour. The situation was hopeless.

Inside, Jake wrestled with the controls. Although he couldn't see outside and none of the instruments were working, including the gyroscopic artificial horizon, his stomach was telling him they were descending quickly. The pounding against the cockpit door had stopped; no doubt the Secret Service had been thrown around the aircraft during its midair collision. Then Jake heard the distinctive sound of gunshots slamming into the door. Someone had managed to brace themselves long enough to try to shoot his way in, a futile gesture, since the door was reinforced against exactly that kind of situation.

Splash Down

Jake couldn't think of a single superpower to help him out of his predicament. He attempted to gather his jumbled thoughts. He could try to teleport the entire crew out en masse, but that would require everybody touching—and he doubted they would give him the chance to explain a plan where they all had to hold hands. He needed to try to stop the flames before they damaged the aircraft any further.

The Raptor pilots thought they were hallucinating when they saw the figure of a young boy *fly through* the burning cockpit and hover alongside Air Force One. Then their secret security briefing came back to mind. He was obviously a *Super*—and because he had come out of Air Force One, they had to assume he was not a hero but a hostile. Then again, he was too small a target to shoot at—if they did attack they risked striking Air Force One.

Jake took stock of the situation. Although it was freezing outside, the thin oxygen was feeding the flames. He needed to smother them with something. He was only half aware that one of the Raptor fighter planes was matching the speed of Air Force One, and flying a few yards above it.

Jake ignored it. He pointed at the burning nose and shot out what he hoped was the right power.

The Raptor pilot was surprised to see a thick layer of ice stream from the boy's hands and cling to the

Boeing's fuselage like snow. The villain zoomed around the nose-diving aircraft and covered the entire front of it with thick ice that killed the flames. Seconds later the ice broke away in large fragments, revealing the black, damaged metal beneath.

It all happened as the pilot was lining up a delicate shot with his M-61 Vulcan Gatling gun. Just a few inches out and he risked blowing a hole in the president's plane. His finger pulled the trigger—just as the shards of jagged ice broke away from Air Force One. Several smashed into his craft at high speed, breaking a hole in the canopy and forcing him to yank back the joystick.

Jake looked up to see tracer fire from the Raptor's Gatling gun arc away from him. The fighter flipped aside, completely out of control. The pilot ejected with a bang that Jake could hear over the rushing wind, and the F-22 Raptor plummeted like a stone. Jake had no wish to tackle the remaining Raptor, so he phased back inside the cockpit.

Jake tried to ignore the ax blade sticking through the door. He had to hand it to the Secret Service, they were persistent. Jake pulled back on the controls and swung the aircraft into a climb before swerving to one side and resuming the descent. He heard thuds and muffled swearing as the Secret Service guys were thrown around.

Splash Down

There was no way Jake could safely land the Boeing on a runway, which was just as well, since he had no idea where the nearest strip of land was. Would ditching it in the ocean be easy? He vaguely remembered that planes were designed to float. He just hoped he wasn't making up *that* particular fact.

Now the horizon appeared level through the side windows, and consumed the front windshield. The white dots that had been scattered icebergs now loomed as big as mountains. Jake judged that it was time to lift the nose and push the throttle forward to lose speed.

The looming icebergs rushed past, so close that the wing tips scraped chunks of ice. The water below was littered with fist-sized ice debris, but Jake had no time to worry about that. He managed to lift the nose with seconds to spare. As the nose rose, the tail struck the ocean. Jake had thought it would be like diving into a swimming pool.

He was completely wrong.

At these speeds hitting the water was like landing on grass. The tail section cracked and the stabilizing fins sheared away as ice smashed into them. But somehow the tail remained attached. The impact forced the front of the Boeing down against the water. . . .

Jake was hurled forward into the control panel. Air Force One belly flopped into the water, but was traveling so fast that it lifted out again and skimmed the ocean like a stone—just clearing a small ice floe before splashing down again.

Jake felt each crunching jar and with it the tortured whine of the engines.

Air Force One skipped for the seventh time before making full contact with the ocean and driving forward like a speedboat, cutting a massive V-shaped wake. The port wing dipped, both engines suddenly cutting into the water with a shrill gurgling scream. The submerged engines acted as a pivot and pulled the aircraft around in an arc.

There was no chance of the stress breaking the wings off. What most people don't realize is that the wings support the *entire* weight of an aircraft during flight. They are the toughest part of any plane.

But when the twin portside engines decided to explode, the resulting conflagration shattered the wing in two and sent an orange mushroom cloud rocketing skyward. Luckily the ocean waves prevented the fires from damaging the body of the aircraft.

The plane skidded sideways in the water for hundreds of yards before smashing to a halt lengthways against an iceberg. Windows shattered, and chunks of ice rained down on the fuselage. The raised starboard wing smashed against the water like a giant flipper and killed the remaining engines.

Splash Down

For a moment there was silence.

Jake opened his eyes, amazed to discover he was alive and elated that he had managed to land, although he had no idea of the extent of the damage. Dull thuds echoed through the plane as emergency exit doors were blown open.

Jake climbed to his feet. Then he took a deep breath and dropped, phasing through the floor.

He appeared in the empty Presidential Suite and ran through the open door. He knew the crew would be abandoning ship. He hurried down a narrow corridor and stopped at the first exit he came to, which happened to be the main entrance. The airstair, a door with built-in steps, had been lowered and already the ocean waves were rolling in. Two bright yellow life rafts bobbed on the frigid waters, crammed with crew. The nearest contained black-suited Secret Service personnel, who seemed to be waiting for Jake. As soon as he poked his head outside, automatic gunfire peppered the fuselage and the wall behind him.

Jake dived across the gap, his shield catching bullets. One eager bodyguard leaped from the raft onto the airstair. Jake saw him scrambling aboard and launched a fireball at him. The flames hit the wall just above the bodyguard's head. The man slipped back down the stairwell and into the ocean. Jake considered sinking the life raft, but that would no doubt condemn the bodyguards to death. And since they weren't Supers, he didn't want to do that.

Jake ran past the galley and through a plush meeting room. He shoved through a partitioned door and into the tail section, where journalists usually traveled. The rear external door was open and a knot of Secret Service personnel were gathered around the president and the secretary of defense.

Jake opened his mouth to speak—and a hail of gunfire slammed into his head. Even though his shield was working, the accumulated bullets still felt like a fist slamming into his nose. He fell onto his back, and was surprised to find he didn't *stop* sliding.

Jake looked around in panic—the aircraft was slowly seesawing as it flooded. The tail rose at an angle, scraping across the iceberg with a sound like fingernails across a chalkboard. Water flooded through the front door, and a mini-wave rolled toward him.

The president and his staff floundered as the Boeing shuddered. They were thrown *away* from the emergency exit as the angle of the floor increased.

Air Force One was sinking.

Freezing water splashed over Jake's head, instantly spurring him on. He jumped to his feet, his boots slipping on the soggy carpet.

"Aw, no!" he cried. Things were getting rapidly out of hand.

Splash Down

He jumped straight up, passing through the ceiling and out over the aircraft. The bird's-eye view allowed him quickly to assess the situation. The front of the aircraft was just under the surface, issuing streams of bubbles. The tail was already twenty feet out of the water, still rubbing against the iceberg. As he watched, it cracked away, falling into the water with a mighty splash.

Three full, yellow, hexagonal lifeboats bobbed away from the wreckage; the bodyguards frantically rowed to a fourth empty boat that was supposed to contain the president.

Jake hovered above, and luckily nobody was paying him any attention. He couldn't deal with an onslaught of bullets. He had to try something, something impossible.

He closed his eyes and felt the superpowers charge through his system. Basilisk, Chameleon, and Mr. Grimm had all told him how special he was—and now was the time to prove it.

Jake couldn't explain how he knew which power to call up, but nevertheless he could feel his fingers pulse. The last time he had used telekinesis had been to push aside the security cameras at Diablo Island. Now he was attempting to lift more than three hundred tons of aircraft.

Inside, the president and his staff had been thrown against a partition wall as water pooled around their feet. Behind them they could see only open sky where the tail used to be. The president was being man-handled toward the exit and was preparing to jump out when the aircraft rocked again, throwing everyone back to the floor. One unlucky bodyguard slipped from the gap in the tail and fell into the icy sea.

Survivors in each raft watched in amazement as the blackened nose of Air Force One suddenly rose from the ocean and the plane leveled out, pulling away from the iceberg.

Then they watched with open mouths as it gradually lifted into the sky, water pouring from every doorway. It rose thirty feet before they became aware of Jake hovering over it, both hands extended and intense concentration etched on his face. One bodyguard took aim with his gun, but his colleague pushed it aside, warning him that shooting the Super would probably cause the aircraft to belly flop back into the ocean.

Jake felt charged with power, stronger than he had ever felt before.

He looked down on the battered aircraft and hoped he could pull off his plan. He'd been told it was impossible—but he was willing to push himself to the limit.

The crew in the lifeboats blinked—and Air Force One vanished in a massive boom. They blinked against the clear sky as the last drops of water fell from nothingness.

The president and his secretary of defense had disappeared.

Splash Down

* * *

Mr. Grimm's footsteps clicked on the polished black marble floor. He walked steadily along a corridor that led from one of the outlying islands to the central land mass. Windows in the arched walls offered views over the island network that would have been spectacular had the island not been smothered in thick mist.

A heavily ornate door stood at the end of the corridor. There were eight such doors circling the chamber, each branded to suit the individual Council members from whose island they led. The door in front of Grimm was etched with curling snakes and spiders. It opened vertically with a whisper. Beyond, the Council chamber was bathed in red light. Despite himself, Grimm hesitated before entering.

The Council of Evil's meeting chamber was a vast dome-shaped room built in the *caldera*, or crater of an extinct volcano. It took a few seconds for Grimm's eyes to adjust to the low light levels. Eight alcoves, bathed in shadows, sat on the perimeter of the chamber. They held thronelike seats for each of the Council members. One alcove was raised above the others, signifying the seat of the Council leader whose decision was, supposedly, final. Then again the position was supposed to be temporary. Henchmen, lackeys, and general administration servants took up the space between the recessed thrones; they formed the functional backbone of the

Council of Evil. Mr. Grimm caught the eye of Ambassador Grutt, head of the Council's uncivil service. The ambassador nodded slightly; he was one of the few people on the islands that Mr. Grimm respected.

The center of the room was taken up by a huge opaque holographic image of the world slowly spinning on its axis. Various splashes of red indicated where villains were gaining territories as governments succumbed to their demands, and in some rare cases, fell completely. Yellow border lines were evenly spaced, marking the individual territories run by each of the Council members. It was in these territories that they would lobby and allow permits that enabled the villains to conduct whatever dastardly scheme they had cooked up. The permit system ensured that no single villain would be in competition with another. Of course, there were always those who did not play by the rules, such as Basilisk, and either the Council would deal with them, or the Hero Foundation would be anonymously tipped off to stop them.

The chamber was overly warm, and Mr. Grimm had to brush away a single drop of sweat that had formed on his pale brow. The atmosphere in the room was oppressive. Malice charged the chamber and it gave Grimm the distinct impression that he had just walked into the hive of some diabolical insect.

The door silently closed behind him, cutting out the

last vestiges of daylight. Grimm took his position with the rest of the administration staff and waited.

The image fizzled then disappeared. Clearly, he had just walked in on the end of a presentation. A plangent voice echoed through the chamber. It had such a melancholy quality that Grimm started feeling his will to live seeping away. It was the current Council leader, Necros.

"Progress is excellent. But I still see that the more established countries are putting up resistance, thanks to the Foundation. That will soon end when the Hero Foundation falls. Already we have a threefold increase in our recruitment process worldwide. Children in particular are signing up to Villain.net in droves."

Grimm knew that without the necessary guidance, those new young villains, like their heroic counterparts, would be nothing more than cannon fodder. But that suited the Council's needs perfectly, although on rare occasions talented stars were discovered.

A deep voice spoke out. White lupine eyes gleamed from one alcove, made all the more alarming by the fact there were two pairs, one above the other. It was the bloodthirsty supervillain known as Fallout.

"Basilisk continues to avoid our bounty hunters and yet you still find him valuable?"

A sibilant voice came from the recess opposite. Mr. Grimm's head did not move, but his eyes swiveled to identify the speaker. He saw only a bulbous green head

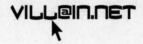

lean forward, housing what he knew to be the terrifying intellect of Professor Mobius.

"We have him to thank for bringing Hero.com off-line. He has brought together a merry little band of villains who have their own grudges against the Council. But he is proving to be quite successful in his efforts. If we allow him to proceed in toppling the Hero Foundation, then I foresee a great victory. Afterward we can punish him for the failed assassination attempt on us all."

"I do not trust him."

"Perhaps you fear him, Fallout?" An angry snarl answered that comment, and Mobius allowed himself a gruff chuckle. "Rest assured that we have Trojan watching him closely."

Another Council member sitting across from Grimm joined in. In the dim light he could just see a large head fanning out at the crown, and four crimson armor-clad muscular arms resting on the throne. The rest of the figure was cloaked in shadows that seemed to cling to him: Armageddon.

"It is Viral I am concerned with. He is a threat to us all. He belongs on Diablo Island. Or better, dead. Worse still, I hear reports that Lord Eon escaped in the prison revolt after Hunter escaped and Basilisk broke in. If this proves to be true, *everybody* is in mortal danger, whichever side they are on!"

Murmurs of agreement filled the chamber.

Splash Down

Mobius raised his hand for silence. "I concur. However, Basilisk still has his part to play. Mr. Grimm, you will be inside the Hero Foundation when Basilisk arrives there?"

"I will be."

"Good. Then you will aid him as much as necessary. Lower the exterior shields to ensure he has no problems on his arrival. Although I am sure that he will try to kill you."

Mr. Grimm gave a formal bow. "It shall be done."

A rapid bubbling noise, which turned into a high-pitched whistle like a kettle boiling, caught everybody's attention. It came from close to Grimm. He turned to see that the alcove had been converted into what looked like, on first glance, a jacuzzi. Inside was a writhing mass of liquid that took a humanoid shape: Abyssal.

"We seem to be forgetting the point of convening today. The boy . . . Hunter. Where is he?"

All eyes turned to the raised seat where the spindly figure of Necros sat. Grimm could smell the stench from here and was thankful the chamber was so dark. Next to him he saw Chromosome lean forward with a calculating look on her face. Grimm knew that the look meant she was coveting Necros's seat as Council leader.

"Chromosome," said Necros with a voice that reverberated with gloom. "You were tasked with tracking the boy down."

Chromosome stepped into the center of the chamber. She walked like a catwalk model and seemed entirely out of place—until the shadows on the floor shifted with faint arachnid forms.

"So far the boy has been elusive. My research has shown it was probably a high-powered member of the Hero Foundation that aided his escape from Diablo Island and is now helping him stay hidden."

She took great delight in soaking up the sudden murmurs that circled the chamber. Mr. Grimm said nothing, but he knew it all to be lies. Most things Chromosome said were. He mused that this must be part of her plan to become Council leader.

Necros stood. "If this is true, who was it? And why?"

"It certainly seems like the Foundation has split views. Maybe a breakaway faction wishes to establish their own operations?"

Further disinformation calculated to throw the Council off Hunter's scent. Chromosome was smiling sweetly.

"Then it must be a plan to overthrow both the Foundation *and* the Council!" cried Fallout, both fists simultaneously thumping his chair arms. "My spies have received reports that Hunter kidnapped the president!"

More clamoring among the Council. Chromosome's eyes met Grimm's and she arched a perfect eyebrow; she obviously hadn't yet heard how successful her plan

Splash Down

had been. Mr. Grimm walked forward and composed himself by not making eye contact with *anybody*.

"It is true. Hunter teleported Air Force One and the president from the Atlantic Ocean."

Gasps of astonishment filled the chamber. A voice to the left caught Grimm's attention. It came from a huge fat man who could crush Grimm to death under his folds of flab if he fell on him. He was called Momentum.

"He teleported the *entire* aircraft? That's impossible!"

Grimm opened his mouth to speak, but stopped when he felt Chromosome's hand on his shoulder. Several spiders crawled around his shins. Grimm tried not to pay attention to them.

"Nevertheless," purred Chromosome, "it appears he did it. Hunter is indeed more powerful than we thought. I shall increase my efforts to locate him."

"Perhaps you need assistance?" said a high voice that sounded as if the speaker was a prim schoolgirl. Chromosome's face momentarily dropped when she heard it, and they all turned to the final Council member. She was Yohg-Shuggor, the Destroyer of Worlds, the Bringer of the Night, the Spawn of the Damned, Eater of the Dead, the Apocalypse Harbinger, and the Shaker of Worlds. But her close friends called her Amy. Her current earthbound form was that of a small girl of about thirteen, with flame-red hair and wearing a plaid skirt.

Chromosome sucked in a deep breath, and the fake

smile covered her face again. "Thank you for the offer, but my powers will be ample enough to track down the boy."

Chromosome met the girl's searching gaze, and she was grateful to turn away when she heard Necros's voice carry through the chamber like a lead weight.

"You should focus all your time on this task, Chromosome. It is the most important of Council business."

Chromosome gave him a terse nod.

"Then I shall see to it at once."

Grimm watched as Chromosome's throne drifted across the floor to meet her. Only when it was close enough for her to sit, did Grimm see that eight metallic spiders' legs propelled it. He shivered, realizing that the throne was *alive*, another mad creation from Chromosome's warped mind. With Chromosome seated, the throne spun around and scurried for the door, the spider entourage following.

"Grimm, come with me," Chromosome commanded.

Mr. Grimm followed her as the door snapped open, relieved to be leaving the dark chamber. He made the mistake of catching Amy's eye on the way out, and for a moment he felt an icy finger stab his brain. Was she trying to read his thoughts? The scowl she gave him no doubt shortened his life span by several years.

He followed Chromosome across the bridge in

silence; a silence made more oppressive as the mist had closed in, allowing only a few yards of visibility. When they had distanced themselves from the Council chamber, her throne pirouetted. In the daylight Grimm could see the throne's metal skin undulate as though it were breathing. The red padded seat resembled a raw liver and he could swear it readjusted to Chromosome's shifting body.

"Where is Hunter?"

Chromosome's delicate tones had been replaced by ice. She glared suspiciously at Mr. Grimm. Grimm's face was blank and unreadable.

"As I said, Hunter teleported straight—"

He didn't see her move, but in the blink of an eye Chromosome was standing in front of him, her slender fingers around his neck. Despite possessing no obvious muscles, she effortlessly lifted him off the floor and held him out over the mist-shrouded balcony. It was a long drop; not that that bothered Grimm because he could fly, but there were *worse* things she could do to him.

"The Council may be employing you, but I am paying you much more. Your loyalty lies with me alone. Understand?"

Grimm tried to nod. A chrome spider had scuttled into his mouth and he couldn't talk.

"Where is the boy?"

The spider ran out of his mouth and perched on his

head. He felt a jolt of pain as the spider pressed two fangs into his forehead, drawing blood. Grimm used all his resolve to keep eye contact with Chromosome.

"Unknown, but he will come to me. He has carried out your wishes so far."

Chromosome regarded him for a few seconds, and then gently lowered him back onto the bridge. Spiders jumped off him and surrounded her as she took her seat. Grimm wiped the blots of blood from his forehead with a white handkerchief. He had seen Chromosome's Legion strip a man of his flesh like a school of piranhas, so he considered his wound a mere graze.

"Ready him for the exchange. The president for information of Psych's location."

"Do you really know where Psych is?"

Chromosome gave a sharp laugh. "Who cares where he is? When Hunter shows, he will be joining me whether he likes it or not. We'll rendezvous some- where I can demonstrate my powers if he feels the need to challenge me. Somewhere that will be the last place the citizens of America will look for their pre- cious leader, right under their noses. Liberty Island."

"New York?" exclaimed Mr. Grimm in surprise. "Isn't that a little too public? And bringing the American president back to his—"

"The president is nothing more than a mascot. It's access to his military might that I want. Then the

Splash Down

Council will have a little uprising when they realize that I have agents in every one of their territories. I will have Hunter under *my* control, doing only my bidding. Who will be left to stop me? Then I will start the world over from scratch. Cast it in my own image."

"Kill everybody?"

"Everything. I have the power to create life from the lifeless."

She tapped a button on Grimm's suit. The plastic rippled as it suddenly grew a stubby pair of wings, detached itself and flew onto Chromosome's hand. Grimm could see that she had indeed created life. The button bug had tiny legs; two probing antenna gently tapped her hand.

"And I have the power to destroy."

She crushed the bug between her thumb and finger.

It was a rare moment, but Grimm was genuinely rattled. He'd had no idea Chromosome was so insane. "You're talking about being a god."

"A goddess," snapped Chromosome tartly. "But not *everybody* will die. Be a good servant, Grimm, and you'll see my new paradise."

Grimm bowed, although he knew without a doubt that Chromosome was raving mad.

"An offer beyond any wealth," he said humbly.

"Yes it is. Tell me when Hunter makes contact. I wish things to start rolling right away. I have much to do."

Grimm nodded and watched her vanish in the mist. Only the faint sounds of her arachnid troop could be heard. He glanced back in the direction of the Council chamber. If he told them about Chromosome's plan, then there would be uproar and they would turn on her in a fight that would lead to open feuding as accusations were thrown and allegiances questioned.

The Council was full of ambitious villains, and not just the eight in power. Minor villains schemed and plotted to one day sit in their place. It was a world of intrigue and backstabbing, originally designed as a democracy, with the Council being voted in. But as soon as Necros became leader and tasted power, he turned it into a dictatorship.

That would not do for Mr. Grimm. He liked to maintain the equilibrium. There was only one weapon he needed to nudge the balance back in the right direction. Jake Hunter.

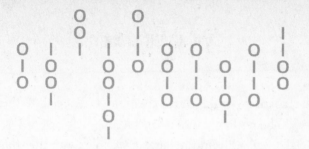

Family Ties

Air Force One dropped three feet to the floor of the hangar when it materialized in Jake's new lair. The resulting thunderclap was so loud that it momentarily deafened everybody on board. The hangar was big enough to house two Boeings. A set of huge closed doors led out to a camouflaged airstrip on a mountain plateau; the doors themselves were disguised to resemble the mountain face.

Jake was impressed that he'd achieved the impossible by teleporting the aircraft, but it had left him weak and trembling. He tried to fight the temptation to log on to Villain.net to feed his cravings, but the desire was just too strong. He briefly wondered if Basilisk had known the enormity of his powers?

He dropped to the floor of the hangar, feeling light-headed. Immediately he dealt with the president, his secretary of defense, and the remaining Secret Service staff by encasing them in a crystalline coating as Chameleon had done to him, briefly, in the shopping mall. Mr. Grimm had suggested the power, saying that the coating would allow them to breathe, but they would be nothing more than statues.

Jake walked from the hangar, wobbled into the stone passageway beyond, and then collapsed.

He awoke in the largest bed he'd ever been in. Judging by the stone walls he was still in the castle—*his* castle, as he corrected himself. At the end of the bed a television was playing a twenty-four hour news channel. The main story was the sudden disappearance of the president while aboard Air Force One. No mention was made of flying villains or superpowers.

Jake sat up in bed, and noticed there was a drip attached to his arm that snaked away to a computer at the side of the bed. The screen showed that the computer had been logged on to Villain.net. It was the same setup Basilisk had used to keep him alive.

He was feeling much better until he noticed that he was still wearing the same clothes. He stank. Here he was, a supervillain with his own Transylvanian castle lair . . . and he couldn't afford clean underwear.

The door opened and Jake felt a little disappointed that there was no spooky creak. Mr. Grimm entered, and Jake noticed the two punctures on his forehead.

"You're awake," he said without preamble. "Feel able to walk?"

"Well, I could use a shower, some clean clothes, and food. But yes."

Family Ties

"Food is being prepared and there are clean clothes in the bathroom."

Jake looked questioningly at Grimm. "Prepared by who?"

Mr. Grimm looked as if he was about to snap a reply, but instead took a deep breath. The tension on his face eased. "Forgive me, times are stressful and I need to be elsewhere. I have hired a servant for you. He's a mute called Igor." Jake grinned and was about to joke about the name, but Grimm continued. "You have fourteen hours before you hand the president and his staff over to Chromosome." Grimm hesitated as though he was about to say more.

"Where? I don't think I can teleport that thing again."

"I will give you the details closer to the time. But you can dispose of the aircraft. Chromosome only wanted it to vanish for shock value." He pointed to the television screen. "And I'm sure you can see you have achieved that."

Mr. Grimm appraised Jake. Although his face didn't register it, his voice had an edge of respect. Not encouragement, like Jake had received from few people other than Basilisk, but genuine respect.

"Nobody has ever achieved what you did. *Nobody.*" Jake felt a warm feeling of pride; it wasn't something he could remember feeling before. "Your powers are greater than even I thought. And I tell you now, people from both sides will ask you to do things you do not wish to."

Jake narrowed his eyes. "Will *you*?"

"I will certainly *urge* you in one direction. Only you can decide what is best."

Jake was surprised. He was expecting flat-out denial from Mr. Grimm, but instead he'd been told what appeared to be the truth. Jake felt the tension in his shoulders relax a little. He nodded toward the computer.

"How long was I hooked up to this for?"

"I found you unconscious when I returned, which was about eight hours ago. The Web site seems to be the only thing keeping you alive right now."

"Do you know what powers I downloaded?"

"While unconscious? Who knows what happened. You have a bond with Villain.net that you need to break before you become a slave to it. And as far as I can tell, you will still have to download powers in the regular way. If you do not, then they seem to become . . . *jumbled*."

"Jumbled? I don't understand."

"Your old friend, Warren Feddle . . . Scuffer. What you did to him was unprecedented."

"I don't know *what* I did to him." Jake's face hardened. "But the idiot deserved it."

"I'm sure he did. But no power exists in the world to do what you did."

Jake sighed. "I know that. Chameleon told me that my body's acting like a . . . chemical lab. I just want to know how to control it."

"That is the question, isn't it?" Mr. Grimm glanced at his watch. "I must leave. Igor will serve you in the kitchen, and then I suggest that you greet your guests and feed them. We don't have to be barbarians."

Igor turned out to be a six-foot-tall thirty-year-old man, with the sort of chiseled good looks that Jake associated with movie stars. All images of a hunch-backed dwarf vanished the moment Igor smiled and laid a five-course meal on the table. Jake had stared at the array of food, enough to feed a football team. It was the only substantial thing he had eaten for more than a month. He felt a wave of sadness once again as he thought about his mother's Sunday lunches. He finished quickly and headed to the hangar.

It took him ten minutes of wrong turns and back-tracking before he got there. Mr. Grimm had taken the president and his secretary of defense out of their crys-talline prisons, and they now sat on chairs to one side of the crippled aircraft. They stood defiantly when Jake entered.

"Hello," said Jake, unsure just what to say to the most powerful non-super man on the planet.

The secretary of defense sprang at him with a waggling finger. "This is an outrage! I demand you return us to the nearest United States embassy at once and hand yourself in for kidnapping the president! How dare you! You're nothing more than a . . . a . . . kid." He finished lamely as he suddenly noticed that was *exactly* what Jake was.

The president stared at Jake with a glimmer of recognition. "I know you. You're . . . "—he racked his memory—"Jake Hunter."

Jake was surprised—but Igor ruined the moment by arriving with a trolley of food and drinks. He barely gave the president, the smashed Air Force One, or the secret service—guards who were still frozen in crystal— a second glance before leaving.

"Help yourself," said Jake. "The beef's excellent. So you know me?"

The president sat down and crossed his legs in what he hoped was a relaxed manner. "I never forget a face that threatens to throw the world off its axis and asks for my air force to hand over its stealth fighters."

It took Jake a moment to remember how the president knew his face. Then it occurred to him. "Ah, the video demand." Events just weeks ago were a distant memory. He wondered if that was a side effect of the superpowers. Basilisk had convinced Jake to deliver a ransom demand to the world's leaders. He had sworn that Jake's face would be digitized, but it seems that was just another of Basilisk's hollow promises.

"Yes, the demand. A ransom that you never got." A defiant smile crossed the president's face.

Jake shrugged and turned to examine the frozen security guards as if they were museum exhibits. "I didn't want any of that. I was being used."

"Used? You were in cahoots with Basilisk! I've crossed swords with that creep before. That makes *you* my enemy, even before you kidnapped me!"

Jake whirled around, his voice raised.

"Basilisk is my enemy too! He used me! He turned me into some superpowered freak. I hate him!"

The president was surprised by the fury in Jake's voice. The president knew all about the world of Supers, and though Jake was just a fourteen-year-old boy, the president knew that Jake was just as dangerous as any dictator armed with weapons of mass destruction.

"That changes nothing, Hunter."

Jake calmed down a little, but began pacing the hangar with his arms behind his back. He stopped in horror as he realized that pacing like that was exactly what Basilisk used to do. He wondered just how much Basilisk had got inside his head.

"Look, I'm really sorry to have to do this to you. Seriously, I am. But it's for a good cause."

"You threaten me, you threaten the country. Scum

like you make the world live in fear for their safety. So forgive me if I don't share your enthusiasm. You do realize that within minutes the marines will burst through that door and kill you?"

Jake smirked. "I don't share *your* enthusiasm about *that*. Nobody's going to be saving you. But on the plus side, I have no intention of harming you. In a few hours you'll be out of my hair when I hand you over to Chromosome."

All pretense of being proud and noble vanished from the president's face the second he heard the name.

The secretary of defense gave a little burble. "Chromosome? You plan to hand us over to that . . . " The word never made it to his lips; he was suddenly too nervous.

Jake watched them carefully. Obviously they were aware of the danger they were in, and the fact they might not live much longer was weighing on their minds. Jake tried not to think about it. He knew he shouldn't get involved. It was like bullying—you never can bully your own friends, you're too close to them. He tried to change the conversation.

"Try and eat. It's not poisoned, I promise."

"Why are you doing this, son?"

Jake looked up to see the president was hunched forward in his chair, studying Jake carefully.

"You wouldn't understand."

Family Ties

"I'm the president of the United States of America, try me."

"Like I said, you wouldn't understand."

The president sat back and folded his arms. "Is that because I'm a politician . . . or an adult?"

Jake smiled slightly. He might as well tell the truth; he had promised himself he was through with liars and lying.

"I'm doing this so that I can get my family back."

"I know that feeling, Jake."

"Sure you do."

"I do. I told you that I crossed paths with Basilisk before. He kidnapped my daughter. If it wasn't for a superhero called Chameleon, I wouldn't have gotten her back alive."

Jake bit his lip. He thought it wasn't the best time to mention that he wanted to kill Chameleon as well.

The president reached for the inside of his jacket—then hesitated. "I'm just reaching for my wallet. There's no gun there."

Jake shrugged. "Wouldn't do you much good if there was."

"Fair point." The president took out his wallet and opened it to show Jake a picture of his wife and two smiling daughters. "That's my family."

Jake took the wallet and stared at the photograph long and hard. He recognized the first family from TV.

"I have a family too," piped up the secretary of defense. "A son and daughter and my wife . . . well, she doesn't really count because I think she's about to divorce me— "

The president kicked him in the shin to silence him.

"We've all got families, Jake. And we all think ours is more important than anyone else's. Fact of the matter is, your family is just as important to you as mine is to me. And if you hand me over to the Council of Evil, forget about how the country will react. It's my family who will suddenly lose their father."

Jake stared at him and regretted getting into a conversation. He handed the wallet back.

"If I let you go, you get your family back. I still lose mine."

"If the Council has taken them, perhaps I can help?"

"I doubt it. My family is free. They just don't remember me. A 'hero' called Psych erased their memories. They don't remember me at all. In fact, they can't even see me."

"That *is* tough." Jake stared at him. The president seemed sincere, but Jake's dad had always told him that the best actor in the world was a politician wanting your vote. "However, I can help."

Jake shook his head and turned away.

"I've already got help." He walked to the door and turned just before leaving. "Please, eat. I'm not the evil dirtbag you think I am. My fight's not with you. You're just a normal guy. I'm out to get the Supers. I'm sorry *any* of this happened. Serves me right for opening spam e-mails."

Jake wasn't at all tired, so he had to find something to take his mind away from thoughts of his family and the fate of the people he held as prisoners in the bowels of his castle.

He ascended the single tower, and looked around his sparse command center. He flicked on a couple of television monitors, which played various news channels. At home he never watched the news, as he didn't care what was happening in the world. But right now he couldn't take his eyes off the screen. There were reports from Tokyo, Chicago, and London about street battles. The footage showed military tanks and ranks of riot police— but never *who* they were actually fighting.

Jake knew though. On another monitor he could see the ticker at the top of Villain.net revealing the news faster than the reporters at the scene. Without heroes to stop them, the villains were running amok. A criminal called Wildfire was playing loud rock music in the streets of Chicago as he caused untold mayhem and derailed an L train. A team of thugs unfortunately named Union Jacks were robbing banks and jewelry stores in London, and somebody with a name Jake couldn't pronounce was toppling buildings in Tokyo.

He tore his eyes away from the screens, flicking one of them on to a loud music channel, and stepped out on the balcony. He leaned on the parapet as he soaked in the view of the jagged mountain peaks. It was night, but the skies were clear, offering a spectacular celestial sight. He remembered stargazing with his dad many winters ago, before he'd grown up into . . . into the obnoxious, ungrateful bully that he'd somehow associated with being "cool." He wondered where his life had all gone wrong. Ordinarily he would have blamed his parents, but now he just couldn't bring himself to.

He was a product of his own mistakes, and he had to live with that. A burning smell caught his nostrils and he looked down to see that his hands were glowing white-hot and burning through the stone parapet. He shook them out immediately. Basilisk had once told him to use his anger to trigger his powers, but now it seemed *any* emotion triggered them. He'd have to be careful in the future.

His cell phone vibrated. It was a text message from Mr. Grimm, with instructions and times to hand over the president. A second one from Grimm arrived on its heels. Jake read it twice to make sure he was reading it right.

CHROMOSOME WILL TRY TO DOUBLE-CROSS

Family Ties

YOU. IF SHE DOES NOT GIVE YOU PSYCH'S LOCATION, THEN DO NOT GIVE HER THE PRESIDENT. IT IS OF UTMOST IMPORTANCE THAT YOU

Jake sighed, that's all there was. Grimm obviously was not a fan of sending abbreviated text messages, otherwise he could have got the whole thing in one text. A third message arrived moments later.

FLEE IF YOU MUST. DO NOT LET HER FOLLOW YOU BACK. DO NOT LET HER HAVE THE PRESIDENT FOR NOTHING. WATCH YOUR BACK!

Jake Googled his destination and made sure he had enough photographic references so that he could teleport there with the president and his entourage. Then he headed down to the hangar to prepare them.

The image of the president's family hung in his head, and Jake felt doubt gnaw at him. If Chromosome was planning to double-cross him, then he was going to get *very* angry.

In the stillness of the Romanian night there appeared to be no activity in the single-spire castle. Chameleon watched from a mountain peak opposite; in his lizard form he was as still as a gargoyle. When he did move, it was like a whisper through the dark. He flew across the valley and latched on to the sheer cliff walls. He could still see the solitary light burning in the tower. There was no sign of movement.

Chameleon had hacked into Mr. Grimm's files at the Foundation. Grimm was a contractor hired to fix problems that the Hero Foundation couldn't or wouldn't, so there was very little in his records other than the meticulously documented reports on the various operations he had performed for the Foundation. This was classified material, and something that Chameleon should not have been privy to. It felt like reading the files from a corrupt government rather than the squeaky-clean Hero Foundation. But he supposed that was what Mr. Grimm was usually hired for—dirty work.

He was annoyed not to find anything incriminating, so he forced himself to read through the files again. This time he noticed a reference to seizing a castle lair from a notorious supervillain Baron Von Gloom, and a photo of the castle itself. Usually a defeated villain's assets would be utilized by the Foundation or sold for a profit.

Chameleon sighed. He remembered reading about the old days when the Foundation would donate such buildings to orphanages and hospitals. How times change, even for the good guys.

Chameleon cross-referenced Von Gloom's castle with the Foundation's main database but drew a blank.

Family Ties

It appeared to be missing. It was such a large oversight for Grimm to make . . . unless it was deliberate. Could Grimm have kept the asset for himself? It was a thin lead, but enough to raise Chameleon's suspicions. He left the Foundation HQ in secrecy and teleported to Romania.

Now that he was here, Chameleon knew he had little choice but to infiltrate the castle and poke around. He glanced down at the flat valley below, and hesitated. It was *unusually* flat. He recalled reading that Baron Von Gloom had a penchant for aircraft—so he guessed that the valley must be an old landing strip.

Chameleon flew headfirst down the cliff and landed gently. The ground was firm beneath his clawed feet, and covered in dirt and brambles. He had guessed right; it was obviously once a landing strip but with nowhere to shelter aircraft. Curious, he turned to examine the sheer wall and began probing around. Villains were a predictable lot, and there was no doubt a—CLICK! A section of the wall pushed inward under his clawed hand and the cliff rolled apart; the seams between the two doors had been artfully blended together.

Now Chameleon could see straight into an aircraft hangar and he braced himself to unleash a fireball. But instead he was greeted by stillness. The hangar was brightly lit, and he was shocked to see the battered carcass of Air Force One. Before Chameleon had left there had been no reports that the president was missing, but he had now been gone for many hours. He resisted the temptation to run in and shout for his old friend.

He quickly searched the hangar and confirmed he was alone, before he turned his attention to the aircraft. His first thoughts that it was a fake were dashed when he explored inside. He'd been invited aboard Air Force One when he had saved the president's daughter. But since governments had strict guidelines that prevented any Super from entering seats of power, he hadn't been invited into the White House. Just in case.

Chameleon's heart sank. The president had been in trouble while he had been poking his nose in restricted Foundation archives instead of doing his job. The next question on his mind was, how did this all link with Grimm? At least it confirmed his suspicions that Grimm was up to no good.

Chameleon sneaked out of the only door, which was partially open, and up a broad, spiral staircase. After several minutes, and with throbbing thigh muscles, he calculated that he must now be in the castle basement. He passed several dark prison cells and looked inside. Empty.

Further investigation took him up another level to the kitchen area, where he could hear a radio playing Romanian songs that reminded him painfully of the European version of *American Idol*.

Family Ties

He poked his head around the kitchen door. It was decked out with modern stainless steel and all the implements needed for a gourmet chef. It had a huge refrigerator, and a massive fire burned in front of an oak table. The aroma of cooked food on the table caught his nostrils and made his stomach rumble.

That noise was the only cue Igor needed. He had been hiding under the table with a meat cleaver in his hands. His instructions had been simple. Defend the castle from any intruders. He leaped out without a whisper.

Chameleon barely managed to duck as the cleaver swished over his head. He retaliated with a punch—which fell wide. Igor was nimble, and tossed the blade into his other hand as he circled the hero.

Chameleon quickly assessed the situation. If the man had any superpowers he would have used them instead of the cleaver, which meant he was just the cook. Chameleon almost laughed. He had dealt with vile supervillains who could tear the flesh off a person with a sonic scream; he had stopped nuclear attacks, earthquakes, and robberies. An ordinary guy posed no problems.

His tail whipped out, aiming straight for the man's face. But Igor easily dodged the overconfident blow and struck out with the cleaver. Chameleon felt a stab of pain as the blade sliced his tail in two. Blood splattered the stainless-steel refrigerator door.

VILL@IN.NET

Chameleon dropped to his knees in agony, and Igor seized his moment of weakness to pounce. This time Chameleon acted in time and unleashed a fireball that plucked the man from the air, mid-leap, and hurled him against a wall rack of utensils. He fell to the floor with a loud clatter, his shirt smoldering. He didn't move.

Right now Chameleon didn't care if he had killed the man or not. He grabbed the end of his tail and squeezed tightly to stem the blood flow. He closed his eyes and willed the pain away. It wasn't easy. But after what seemed like an eternity the pain faded and a new section of his tail started to grow a few inches at a time. It wasn't a superpowered healing factor. Like most common lizards, Chameleon had the ability to regenerate his tail if it was severed, though of course his regenerated much quicker, and it was still a painful process.

Only after he was whole again did he check on the cook. He felt a weak pulse. Satisfied the man was alive, he prowled around the rest of the castle.

It didn't take him long to discover that, aside from the cook, the place was empty. In a bathroom, he found a stack of old smelly clothes that he recognized as belonging to Jake Hunter, and a television playing the news. In a couple of minutes Chameleon was fully briefed on the rapidly changing world situation, and the fact that the president was missing. That confirmed his suspicions: Grimm was working for the enemy—at the very least he was colluding with Hunter. Chameleon decided not to report his discovery to the Foundation just yet. He would need hard evidence to convince the Foundation's leader. He had to catch Grimm red-handed.

He finally climbed the castle's tower and found himself in what passed for a command center. His eyes were immediately drawn to a computer screen showing pictures of Liberty Island. Chameleon scoured the Internet history and found that was all Hunter had been searching for. He decided that must be where he was taking the president.

He glanced at the computer's clock and prayed that he could make it there in time to save him.

Freedom and Liberty

Jake stared up at the floodlit back of the Statue of Liberty Enlightening the World, more commonly known as the Statue of Liberty. He stood in the circular walkway surrounding it, and even from more than three hundred feet away he had to crane his neck to take in the full statue.

Liberty Island was empty. Nobody patrolled it at this time of night except a few coast guard vessels. The president stood with him, gazing up. His Secret Service crew were still encased, and Jake had had enough of the secretary of defense's complaining and had zapped him into a crystalline statue too.

"It was a gift from the French, you know," said the president when he regained his balance after the sudden teleportation. "A symbol of liberty and freedom."

Jake didn't respond. He nervously glanced northeast to the battery of lights that formed the Manhattan skyline, and behind him, at the shores of New Jersey. He felt like an open target here on a small island in Hudson Bay.

Freedom and Liberty

The president pointed to the irregular eleven-star foundation and narrow granite plinth the statue stood on. Jake felt as if he was with a tour guide. "The height's all an illusion though. That base is higher than the statue itself. Still . . . she's a wondrous sight to behold."

Jake looked sidelong at him. He'd been mulling over Mr. Grimm's message—Chromosome was not to be trusted and would certainly betray him.

"You should go."

The president stared at him incredulously. "What? Are you kidding?"

"No, seriously. Get out of here. This is all wrong. Chromosome has no intention of helping me track down Psych. She just wanted me to do her dirty work."

The president still made no move. "You'll forgive me if I don't believe you."

Jake turned to him. "Go back to your family." He nodded his head toward the frozen entourage. "Them too. This is not your fight."

The president looked at him long and hard. "We're on my country's soil. That makes it my fight."

Jake's response never made it to his lips. The water in front of the statue erupted as a circular Council of Evil craft rose from the bay and silently drifted across the island, dripping water like rain as it landed next to the statue. The ramp unfolded from the belly and Jake tensed, hissing at the president.

"Run! Get out of here!"

This time the president heeded his words and darted for cover in the trees. Jake suddenly remembered everybody else was still frozen.

Too late to deal with that now.

Chromosome walked down the concourse toward him, a sea of metal spiders glinting around her feet.

"That's far enough, Chromosome!"

She stopped and folded her arms, looking relaxed and amiable. She studied the president's frozen entourage lining the circular plaza.

"Where is the president, Hunter? I saw him on my monitors when we landed. Is he hiding? Afraid of me?"

"If you know he's here, then tell me where Psych is."

Her hesitation was enough for Jake to know he had been duped. "What you achieved, Hunter, was nothing short of a miracle. Some of your powers have evolved beyond what anybody has ever seen before. You are truly a force to be reckoned with. Why not join me? With our combined strength we could get rid of the Council, the Foundation, and all these warring nations. We could eradicate all life on this planet and start the world again. A new Garden of Eden, just you and me creating life that only *we* think is worthy."

This level of madness surprised Jake. He'd heard about overthrowing the Council from Basilisk, and he didn't care about that—although the Council was becoming a thorn in his side, and he would have to deal with it sooner or later. But restarting the world . . . Though the more he thought about it the more it made sense. Just him and Chromosome, a perfect partnership. They would be . . .

Jake shook his head, clearing away the rose-tinted image conjured by Chromosome's beguiling voice. "You want to play God!"

Chromosome smiled. "And why not? Think about it, Hunter. We'll do a better job. You and I. A fresh new world."

Jake had a warm feeling when she spoke, and he could clearly see a utopia crafted by them both. But he closed his eyes, suspecting that Chromosome had some kind of charm power, something that made men susceptible to her demands. He wasn't going to fall for that.

Eradication of *all life* was what she was suggesting. That was *pure* evil.

This is where years of never listening to his sister would finally come in handy. He could just tune Chromosome out.

"I'm only interested in finding Psych. We had a deal. Where is he?"

"Japan . . . or was it France? Ah, I remember now, he was last seen in the Big Apple, just over there. Or was that Egypt? You know . . . I just can't remember such trivia. If you don't have the decency to listen to my offers of power, then," her honey tones returned, "just give me the president. Where is he?"

Jake saw her head snap toward the trees lining the concourse, and realized that *he* was pointing in the direction the president had run. The subtle tones in her voice must have unconsciously persuaded him to raise his arm. The Legion skittered in that direction.

"No!" Jake launched a fireball at the carpet of bugs. The blast was so severe it gouged a crater into the red-brick concourse and sent the arachnids flipping through the air.

"My Legion!" screamed Chromosome.

Jake turned on her. He didn't know the full extent of her powers, but he wasn't willing to give her the opportunity to use them. He threw another fireball that blasted the ground—but she nimbly cartwheeled aside. When the smoke had cleared, Jake could see that her Legion had reformed and were charging toward him.

He had no time to react before the horde of chrome spiders surrounded him, scuttling up his legs and burrowing into his clothes. He felt hundreds of pin-pricks across his body as they bit him, and he prayed that they weren't poisonous. The onslaught of so many tiny attacks was much worse than anything he'd encountered before and he dropped to his knees screaming, only to have one of the metal spiders crawl into his mouth.

Jake's entire body suddenly flared with a bright green radioactive wave, streamers peeling away from him in a ghostly corona. The Legion was struck, some melting on the spot, others flung across the island. Jake roared and swung the green blast at a startled Chromosome. It was as if a solid weight had struck her. The villain was thrown nearly five hundred feet before slamming down just below the three arches on the statue's pedestal. Stonework cracked around her.

Jake used the lull to unfreeze the president's men. The Secret Service guys acted immediately and drew their sidearms, firing a dozen shots at Jake. He wasn't expecting that. His force field caught the shots, but the impacts made him reel backward.

"Stop shooting! You're free! The president went that way, make sure he gets off this island in one piece!"

The group hesitated, clustering around their only other important charge, the secretary of defense. One weaselly man chirped up. "You heard him! Let's go!"

They ran for cover among the trees. When Jake turned back to Chromosome he saw that she was pushing herself away from the crumpled stonework, assisted by numerous long insect legs that had unfolded from her rib cage and now pushed against the plinth. Free, she dropped thirty feet onto the star-shaped foundation and advanced.

Jake hoped that flying was not one of her abilities and would be his advantage. He took to the air and flew full speed into her. He grabbed her waist and they slammed into the corner of the plinth, knocking gray stones loose.

When he looked back up at Chromosome he didn't recognize the face. The perfect features had warped into a hideous and fanged snarling beast with mottled black skin. Her hands had become clawed talons; the insect legs protruding from her back were actually double-jointed and folded around to the front, gripping Jake in a tight bear hug. He felt and heard a rib crack.

"How dare you challenge me, boy!" she screeched in an unrecognizable voice.

Without being aware of what he was doing, Jake's body enveloped itself in a radioactive aura and he smelled burning flesh. It was Chromosome's. She screamed and released him. Jake shot straight in the air and landed on the tarnished green copper base of the statue to catch his breath.

He saw an emergency flare go up from the west pier and hoped that it was the president signaling for help. Across Hudson Bay he saw a coast guard cutter swing around, its searchlight focusing on the pier, highlighting a group of figures.

When he looked back down he saw the remains of Chromosome's legion scuttling up the plinth. Chromosome herself was writhing as something grew from her back with the sickening sound of crunching bone and tearing flesh. She was *evolving* the limbs she needed to fight Jake.

He backed away, stumbling around to the front of the statue as his injured body regenerated. He was feeling unusually exhausted, and he found it difficult to catch his breath. He backed into a giant chain protruding from the statue's feet. It took him a second to realize that it was part of the statue, a feature that couldn't be seen from the ground. He remembered learning in school that it symbolized the broken chains of repression. He glanced farther down at the viewing balcony that ran around the top of the stone plinth and considered hiding inside the statue.

Then he saw the silver flurry of the Legion scuttling up. He tried to fly, but managed only a few yards—he was too weak to climb any higher. He latched onto the side of the statue like a spider and looked down.

The Legion was reproducing around the feet of the statue like bacteria. One spider would pull itself apart to reveal another. Then he saw Chromosome. She was still at the base of the plinth, but now Jake could see that the protuberances on her back were transforming into wings, growing out larger and larger. She experimentally flapped them like a baby bird.

Jake scurried up the front of the statue to get away from the monstrosities. The copper folds of Liberty's gown made progress difficult. He was halfway up when he heard a clanging sound like a metal barrel being pelted by stones. When he looked down he saw the entire base of the statue had turned silver as the Legion's members scuttled up in pursuit. The Legion had also changed form, morphing into a combination of a spider and a scorpion. Curved tails quivered in anticipation of the kill.

Jake headed sidelong to the wide surface offered by the book in Lady Liberty's left hand. He caught his breath and wondered why he felt so weak.

A quick look around revealed that the coast guard cutter was speeding toward the pier and a swarm of helicopters was buzzing in from the opposite side.

The Legion flooded around him and Jake unleashed his radioactive blast. Most of them were flung aside or melted on the spot. The energy was so intense that it ripped through the hollow copper bodywork of the statue and severed the iron structural beams beneath. The sound of groaning metal reverberated through the statue. Jake stopped in horror, aware that he was defacing a national treasure.

Freedom and Liberty

The break in his attack was enough to give ten creatures a chance to climb onto the smooth surface of the statue's book. Jake's fingers gripped the ruts of the engraving on the book beneath him as the scorpion tails extended and lashed around both his legs, pulling him down the slope. Another positioned itself at his head, the tail suddenly transforming into a spike that struck at his face.

Jake jerked his head aside, but felt the spike slice his cheek and puncture the copper. Though his shield prevented him from getting hurt by explosions, bullets, or other dangers, it was useless against this attack. It offered zero resistance against a slower-moving sharp blade. On top of that, Jake was blinded as several spotlights picked him out when the helicopters neared. He caught sight of a jumble of letters on the side of one chopper and realized that they were news crews. They buzzed around him like flies.

Jake no longer cared that he might be recognized. He picked up the critter near his face and crushed it with his superstrength. After brief resistance it was like smashing an egg, and gloopy innards covered his hand. He had no time to feel sick. He blasted the two Legion creatures climbing up his legs, then managed a short flight up to the statue's crown, where he had to rest again. The searchlights took a few seconds to find him as they weaved across Lady Liberty.

A rustle of leathery wings caught his attention and Chromosome rose into view, mighty batlike wings beating to keep her airborne.

"What's the matter? Feeling weak? Did you not know that I have the ability to negate your powers or evolve myself to fight you in *any way* I need?" Chromosome knew that the effects only lasted for a minute, and could only affect a handful of powers at any one time. But that was not a weakness she would admit to.

Jake lashed out a stream of green energy. It flowed like colorful ribbons, just missing Chromosome, who twisted aside. But it struck one of the helicopters. The tail rotor blew off and the chopper spun out of control. The other news choppers banked aside, relocating to safer distances. The helicopter splashed down into the black water below.

"If I can't have you join me, I'll see if your corpse can offer any assistance to my cause. And I'll still take the president! You lose either way."

She swooped toward the western jetty. Jake glanced down; one of the news helicopters had fixed its beam on the surviving crew of the crashed chopper, who were treading water.

Jake gritted his teeth. Chromosome may be able to nullify his powers, but Jake's were stronger than she imagined. He leaped like a diver off the crown and willed his flying power to take hold.

Freedom and Liberty

Instead he plummeted toward the earth like a rock. She had even negated his ability to fly.

The president watched the coast guard vessel bank around to dock with the L-shaped pier. He turned when he heard the helicopter crashing. Seconds later a winged monstrosity swooped across the island toward him. The Secret Service team had spotted the danger too. The president was tackled roughly to the floor as they threw themselves in front of him, guns blazing.

Bullets hit Chromosome, but they had no effect. She soared in low and plucked one of the Secret Service men into the air. She struggled for altitude with the increased weight—then threw him to the ground. The president looked away to avoid the upsetting sight. When he risked a glance back he saw that Chromosome was swooping in again. This time the coast guard crew, armed to deal with any terrorist attacks, unleashed machine guns on her. Again they had little effect. Time seemed to slow as Chromosome's screaming jaws, lined with jagged teeth, bore straight for the president.

BLAM! A fireball hit Chromosome like a sledgehammer and threw her against the military boat with such force the craft rocked in the water and she tore a hole through the steel deck.

The president looked around, expecting to see

Jake—instead he was looking at somebody else, hovering in the air. The president's eyes widened with relief.

"Chameleon!"

"Mr. President! Sorry I'm late."

Two coast guard crew members were thrown off the deck as Chromosome heaved herself out of the gash in the vessel. Her eyes narrowed when she spotted the hero.

"You! You will die here!" she screamed. Her muscles cracked as she increased mass right in front of them—doubling her size in seconds.

Chameleon expected an attack from her—what he didn't expect was the horde of surviving Legion that suddenly ran out from the undergrowth. They fused together in a bubbling mass of flesh that formed a single tentacle. Anchored to the ground, it whipped around Chameleon's waist, plucking him from the air.

Chromosome turned to face the president, oblivious to the shots still being fired by the Secret Service guys.

"Now, Mr. President, you will come with me."

"I'd rather die!"

"That can be arranged."

With heavy footfalls, Chromosome climbed onto the pier. The wood cracked underfoot. The president and his retinue began to run back to the island—but they stopped when they saw a massive shape flying toward them. Once more the president was wrestled to the ground by his entourage as a huge disk-shaped craft shot over their heads.

Chromosome watched in amazement as she saw her Council of Evil shuttle being hurled at her like a discus. It smashed into her with colossal force, ramming her back into the coast guard ship. The collision was so violent that the shuttle exploded around Chromosome, pinning her to the side of the boat. The combined weight rolled the cutter over with a massive splash. Chromosome's screams turned into gurgles as the bright red keel of the boat was revealed when the boat flipped completely over.

The president looked back to the end of the pier to see Jake wiping his hands after the incredible throw. Jake gave him a brief nod.

"You okay?"

Before the president could answer, there was an explosion from Chameleon and the Legion tentacle was blown into its component spider pieces, each one aflame and scuttling randomly around before dying.

"Mr. President! Down!" yelled Chameleon as he unleashed a fireball at Jake.

"Wait a minute—" Jake started, but the fireball punched him through a line of trees, the boughs catching fire. Chameleon ran in pursuit.

Jake propped himself up on his elbows in time to see Chameleon hurl another ball of flame. He didn't have

time to move. It felt as if a bomb had gone off in front of his face. He was blown nearly three hundred feet back against the base of the Statue of Liberty.

Chameleon hesitated as a police helicopter circled around, stabbing its searchlight on him. He gestured frantically toward the president. The pilot must have understood because the searchlight then fixed on the president and his group.

Jake saw the police helicopter land across the island and knew the president would be taken safely on board. He turned to see Chameleon flying down the concourse toward him. He also became aware that he was no longer feeling weak now that Chromosome was out of the picture. He saw flames burst from Chameleon's hands—and he launched himself straight up to avoid them. His flying power had returned.

Jake corkscrewed around the statue to make himself less of a target. Chameleon flew in pursuit, hurling small volleys of fireballs that hit the statue harmlessly.

"You made your last mistake, Hunter!"

"I don't think so," Jake shouted back—then immediately regretted opening his mouth when he realized how stupid that comment was.

Jake reached the Statue of Liberty's head and landed before he fired straight down on Chameleon. It was a radioactive strand that punched Chameleon forcibly onto the statue's right shoulder. Chameleon rolled across the copper shell, slamming into the raised arm that held the torch aloft, and prevented him from falling off.

"I was coming for you next, Chameleon!" Jake ran to the edge of the crown to look down on his target, who was groaning softly. "There's no way you're taking me back to Diablo Island to be your guinea pig."

"Who said anything about bringing you in alive? You've proved too much of a threat for that. I'm going to have to kill you."

Jake felt uneasy. It was all very well for a villain like Chromosome to threaten his life, but Chameleon was a hero, somebody who had just helped rescue the president. It didn't seem *right* for him to say that. Once again Jake felt the line between hero and villain blur.

He dropped down onto the shoulder and walked toward Chameleon. This close, he could see Chameleon was hit pretty badly, and bleeding from a burn wound to his left arm.

"After what you did to me and my family—"

"What? I saved them from you! They are leading a much happier life now that you're not around, Hunter."

Jake's anger snapped and his bullying instincts took over. Chameleon was weak and injured—a perfect target.

Jake unleashed electrical bolts from his fingers. Jagged lightning racked Chameleon's body and he howled in pain.

"Stop!" he pleaded.

Jake had heard it all before, a hundred times in the school yard. He blasted Chameleon again. The helicopters were still flying around, fixing them with searchlights and camera lenses. Then one of the searchlights suddenly peeled away—focusing on *something* heading toward them. Jake saw it and was frozen to the spot in astonishment.

It was the coast guard vessel. Thrown at them by some Herculean force.

The twenty-foot cutter missed its mark, and the aluminum-hulled boat smashed through the back of Liberty's head, tearing it in half and ripping the face off in a mass of bent metal as the vessel arced down toward the bay—narrowly missing a helicopter. It splashed in the water and immediately sank.

Both Jake and Chameleon looked back to see the enormous winged form of Chromosome bearing down on them. Without hesitation they both fired at the villain. One enormous fireball and stream of radioactive energy hit her full in the chest and she dropped from the sky.

Chameleon leaped to his feet and sneakily unleashed a fireball at Jake, who was standing next to him, watching Chromosome's descent. Jake plowed into the statue's fragmented neck and bounced off.

Jake caught himself in flight and yo-yoed back up in

time to see Chromosome land on the back of the statue, claws gouging metal as she lumbered up like a mutant King Kong.

Chameleon leaned over the edge of the shoulder and fired down, his blast missing Chromosome's face. Jake circled around and almost ran into the whirling blades of a news chopper. He fired from the opposite side of the statue—his fireball tore one of Chromosome's wings in two and she howled in rage, flapping the jagged stump.

Chameleon turned and fired at Jake, but this time he was ready and bobbed out of the way of the shot.

"You idiot!" screamed Jake.

Then he fired a small blob of radioactive energy at Chameleon, who sidestepped it.

Chromosome made use of the distraction and a pair of intense blue laser bolts shot from her eyes. One caught Chameleon and sent him flying off the statue, while the other punctured a massive hole in Liberty's right arm.

The arm, carrying the weight of the gilded torch, swayed, and then it snapped away and fell across the remains of Lady Liberty's head.

Chromosome pressed herself against the back of the statue as the arm passed close by and smashed the rear viewing balcony on the plinth.

Chameleon and Jake zoomed around the statue, almost flying into each other. This time they turned their combined energies on Chromosome and fired.

From the choppers it was impossible to see what happened. The blaze of light was so intense that everybody had to look away.

Jake was stunned by the strength of the blast from his own hands, and he had to shake his fingers to get rid of the pins and needles that ran through them. Both his and Chameleon's shot bored into Chromosome. She shrieked, her good wing on fire.

The Statue of Liberty pitched forward. It moved slowly, like a drunkard falling. The one-hundred-fifty-foot tall Lady Liberty toppled from her plinth—and two hundred and fifty tons smashed into the foundations below, splitting in half.

"Oh my God!" cried Chameleon.

Jake swooped low but couldn't see Chromosome. "Where'd she go?"

He landed on the grass in between the two huge sections of the statue. Jake spun around to see Chameleon standing behind him with a twisted grin.

"Good-bye, Hunter."

Chameleon had his hands raised, but Jake was looking *beyond* the hero—at the giant figure of Chromosome standing over him wielding a broken piece of the statue. She brought it down with crushing force on Chameleon.

Jake reacted without thinking and fired a fine crystalline beam at the hero. Chameleon was instantly encased as Chromosome hit him. It was like driving a nail into the ground—the solidified Chameleon was pushed into the grass by the impact.

"If anyone's going to kill him, it's going to be me," shouted Jake.

Chromosome locked eyes with Jake and raised her makeshift club again. "You should have joined me!"

Jake used one hand to telekinetically bat the statue fragment out of Chromosome's grasp, while simultaneously blasting a fireball from his other hand. He had never launched *two* attack powers before, nor had he seen anybody else do it. He felt himself weaken from the effort.

Chromosome was not expecting the blast and was propelled against the statue's torso with a dull clang. The helicopter searchlights illuminated the area and Jake leaped forward, hands raised to shoot again.

Chromosome was lying on the ground, groaning. The giant insect legs unfolded from her back with a loud crack as she tried to get up. Her own arms and legs flailed uselessly. There was no way she could stand. Despite the danger, Jake couldn't help but laugh out loud. He was reminded of a flipped beetle trying to right itself.

Chromosome hissed at Jake and pathetically scuttled off toward the trees. Jake hesitated. From his angle it looked as though a giant beetle was carrying her.

Chromosome suddenly teleported away and Jake sagged with relief.

He used his telekinetic force to raise the frozen Chameleon from the ground. His nemesis seemed unharmed, despite Chromosome's blow. Ironically Jake's actions had saved the life of the hero who wanted to kill him, and the hero he wanted dead.

Jake laid his hands on Chameleon and teleported away from the destruction of Liberty Island as the helicopters surrounded them.

1730
10
10
000
0
0
10
00
0
10
10
0
1
1
00
00
10
0

The Race Begins

The stone bounced from Chameleon's head with a soft ping and clattered with the others in a small pile by his feet.

Jake stared at his nemesis, housed beneath the thin amber-colored sheen. He could see that Chameleon's face was contorted in a snarl and his entire body was angled to unleash a fireball. When Jake had teleported back to the castle he had positioned Chameleon like an ornament, in the corner of the spacious lounge. He had been sitting on the sofa, idly throwing small stones at Chameleon for half an hour as he tried to relax. He soon drifted asleep.

He woke up an hour later to discover that Igor must have been in and left him a steaming cup of tea, and thoughtfully, a fresh pile of stones to pelt at Chameleon. Every muscle in Jake's body ached, and he was thankful for the sugary liquid that helped him focus his senses. The battle with Chromosome had been brutal, and still he hadn't defeated her. Just like he hadn't defeated Scuffer. The thought of facing either monster again made him shudder. But at least his conscience felt lighter now that he had freed the president and his staff. People were not in his line of fire. Just superhumans.

Jake wondered if his approach of doing this alone was the right one. Mr. Grimm had proved that allies were useful. Jake's experience with his so-called friends betraying him in Russia had taught him that trust was hard to come by. But what if he teamed up with some of the bigger sharks? The Hero Foundation wouldn't trust him at all . . . but the Council of Evil might. They were out to capture him, but if he pretended to help them, in return using their forces to wipe out the heroes he despised . . . then he could ultimately turn on the Council from the inside. . . .

It was an attractive idea, but Jake brushed it aside. He worked better on his own.

At least the experience had delivered Chameleon to him. Jake had daydreamed about exacting revenge on the hero for the punishment he'd put him through on Diablo Island, and for making Psych erase his family's memory. While he was in prison, Jake had fantasized about killing the scaly creep in a variety of original ways, but now that Chameleon was in his hands he just couldn't bring himself to do it. Perhaps keeping him as a permanent statue would be punishment enough? He wondered if Chameleon was still awake beneath the crystal, conscious of every passing second. That would be a living hell. Especially if he had an itch to scratch.

All he needed now was Basilisk and he could start a collection.

He mulled that idea over. It wasn't too bad . . .

The room suddenly began to swim around him, and the tea mug fell from his hand and shattered on the floor. Jake steadied himself by gripping the sofa, and closed his eyes. The dizziness passed, but left him feeling weak. He experimentally raised his hand and saw that it was shaking. He needed to power up.

When he had returned from Liberty Island, Jake had made a conscious decision not to jump immediately on to Villain.net and load up with powers to quench his need. He knew he was too dependent on them, like a junkie needing a fix, and he was determined to wean himself off. But it wasn't working. The longer he delayed recharging, the worse he felt. After he had won back his parents he resolved to find some cure for this addiction. Then he would find Basilisk. His to-do list was growing ever longer.

Jake found it very difficult to walk up the spiral staircase to his command tower. Midway up he stopped to catch his breath and realized he was wheezing like an old man.

He finally made it, slumped into a swivel chair, and closed his eyes. He must have nodded off for another half an hour because he awoke with a nervous jolt and a wave of nausea. Reluctantly he stared at the computer screen displaying Villain.net and selected the first two powers he saw. He didn't care what they were, although he was beginning to recognize some of the icons and knew one power was teleportation—always handy. He decided to choose half the number he usually downloaded in an effort to try to reduce his habit. When they flowed into him he felt immediately refreshed.

Now alert, he checked the Villain.net news banner. It mentioned nothing of his clash with Chromosome, but it did mention the good news that Chameleon was missing.

Jake racked his brain. There had to be a way of tracking down Psych. Poking around Villain.net eventually yielded some information when he uncovered entire files on superheroes, including their powers, stomping grounds, and weaknesses. Very useful, except the entry on Psych was simply labeled: MEMBER OF THE JUSTICE FEDERATION. When Jake searched for files on that team he was taken to a page that declared the superhero group had disbanded.

"Great." Jake moaned aloud. It was obvious that Chromosome had no idea where Psych was either, but it occurred to him that if she wanted to get Jake, then all she had to do was find Psych first. She had probably

The Race Begins

returned to the Council of Evil after their clash to nurse her wounds, and he was certain she had more resources available to track down Psych than he had. How could he prevent her from interfering again? Further confrontation was something Jake didn't relish.

Then he had an idea. It was childish and simple, the kind of thing that made the troublemaker inside him laugh. He'd frame her. A quick search across Villain.net revealed a contact e-mail to report any intelligence. Like the Web site itself, it wasn't a straightforward e-mail address, but it would do.

Jake couldn't stop smiling as he typed the message, paying attention to the spelling in order to make it as professional as possible before he hit "send." He took a deep breath, feeling very pleased with his devious scheme. He just hoped that e-mail was delivered to the right person.

His cell phone suddenly rang and he snatched it up, expecting to hear Grimm's voice.

"Yeah?"

"Jake?"

Jake sat bolt upright in his seat. It was Lorna. He unconsciously ran a hand through his hair to smooth it out.

"Lorna, hi. How're you?" He couldn't think of anything else to say.

"Good. I saw I missed a call from you and, I . . . um . . ."

"It's okay. Wasn't anything important." He immediately regretted saying that. "Where are you? Your voice sounds echoey."

"I'm in . . . the hospital."

"You okay?" Jake realized he was truly concerned.

Lorna laughed. "I'm fine! I'm just visiting a friend."

"I'd come and catch up with you but I'm . . . uh, stuck doing something."

"Oh." There was a long pause. "Not to worry."

Jake wasn't convinced she meant that. "Give me a couple of days to finish things up, and maybe we can go out again?"

"I'd like that. I was thinking about popping by your house—"

"No!" He sounded a little too harsh. "Not yet."

"Your parents still mad?"

"You know what adults are like."

He looked around the room in search of something to say that didn't involve superpowers or kidnapping the president. He caught a report on the news right at the end after the stories about global conflict and war, a silly one designed to "lift your spirits."

"I just saw on the Internet that yaks have prevented those space tourists from lifting off in Kazakhstan. Says herds of them had to be cleared from the launch pad. Must be great flying into space. Maybe we should go to Kazakhstan and give it a try?"

The Race Begins

"Yeah, my brother and I were talking about that," Lorna said, laughing at the absurdity of it. "But yaks? Jake, you're starting to sound funny."

Jake blushed. "Yeah. Sorry."

"Listen, I have to go. Looking forward to catching up with you in a few days, though. Take care."

"You too."

He heard the line go dead and stared at the phone. What was he talking about yaks for? He flicked the TV off, feeling stupid and completely uncool. He could have talked about *anything*, but chose the most irrelevant, stupid subject he could.

What use was that snippet of news to anybody?

Chromosome sat on her mobile throne, which glided through her cavernous chamber. She had crafted her lair by rearranging and fusing the atoms of the rocky island around her to produce a living, breathing room. It was like sitting in the mouth of some enormous predator, with glistening columns that stretched from floor to ceiling and were never in the same place on repeat visits. A warm breeze flowed through as though the room were gasping for breath. There was a constant sound of dripping slime, and the shadowless illumination came from the walls themselves.

Her back was still painfully throbbing from where

Jake had blown her wing off. It's great being able to grow extra body parts, but if they're damaged, they still hurt like crazy. On the plus side, once Chromosome had created a new set of limbs, the instruction would be embedded in her DNA. That meant she could create the wings much faster in the future, just as she had done with the extra insect limbs and doubling her size—all residuals from previous adventures.

The loss of her Legion pained her in other ways. It took time to create such perfect little creatures that could morph into different shapes for whatever task was at hand. It was like having a walking Swiss Army knife. Luckily she had left a few dozen of her Legion behind to guard her lair.

Like the other Council members, Chromosome had abandoned her old lairs and hideouts, and moved to one of the islands circling the Council chamber. Each island was uniquely designed to suit its occupant, and on windy days she could smell a sickening decomposing scent from Necros's headquarters.

A soft, monotone voice echoed around the chamber, as though the room itself were speaking—which was a possibility.

"Ambassador Grutt has arrived to see you."

Chromosome frowned. The Council had ambassadors who could move freely from island to island to solve problems and make sure the Council functioned efficiently. Although they were just ordinary humans, paid a great deal of money, they had diplomatic immunity and, in theory, could take Council members down for their actions. They seldom visited unannounced.

Chromosome sat upright, her injured wing-stub folding flawlessly into her back with a crunch of bone and muscle. She summoned a small drinks stand from the corner of the room, which glided over like a high-speed snail, leaving a trail of slime.

"Enter," she commanded as she poured herself a drink.

The doors to her chamber silently pulled open. Ambassador Grutt entered wearing the formal crimson robes of office. His face dropped slightly as he entered the chamber; he'd never been here before. The doors closed behind him, giving him the unnerving feeling that he had just walked through a heart valve.

He was a portly man, built from too much of the good food and drink that was readily available at the Council. He had a deep tan, which was not surprising given the island's tropical location, and constantly shifting eyes. He briefly dipped his head in greeting.

"Chromosome, thank you for admitting me."

"As if I had a choice, Ambassador," Chromosome said coolly. She hated the servants and bureaucrats who filled the Council's ranks. She decided they would be one of the first things she would get rid of when she rose to power. She would replace them all with computers. "What do you want?"

Grutt wrung his hands nervously. He thought he could see the walls and columns lean slightly in, as though the room were contracting.

"It has come to my attention that you may be plotting Machiavellian operations against the establishment."

Chromosome blinked at him in surprise. Another thing she hated was the ambassador's bombastic way of speaking.

"If by establishment you mean the rest of the world, then yes. That's why I am here. As we all are."

More wringing of the hands.

"We received an anonymous tip-off that your schemes involve terminating key Council members so as to elevate your own position."

Chromosome glared at him, her mind racing for a suitable answer. Her remaining Legion appeared from the shadows and surrounded Grutt, obeying her every telepathic command.

"Your source is confusing my plan to use the president of the United States."

"Ah, yes," said Grutt as he nervously eyed the Legion around him. "The president. An unfortunate blunder."

Chromosome's hand balled into a fist with an audible crunch. Her eyes narrowed. "It was no *blunder*. It was a perfect plan that went awry through lack of Council support."

"You never asked for any support."

"Nevertheless, it should have been offered. Is that all you have to say? Some rambling false accusations? Leave me."

The ambassador held his ground, his voice quivering with nerves. "That is not all. Your failure with the president raised the question of why it appeared you were working with Hunter?"

"Are you crazy?" Chromosome stood up and began circling him. "In the chamber it was Necros himself who asked me to find the boy. And you dare lay suspicion on me for doing my job?"

Her voice rose, echoing through the room. It was so menacing, Grutt involuntarily closed his eyes and clenched his fists.

"It was the external e-mail we received—"

"An e-mail?" Chromosome exclaimed, genuinely surprised. She had been wondering who could have betrayed her from within the Council. But now she had somebody from outside to contend with.

"Y-yes, an e-mail came in . . . " Grutt was beginning to lose his nerve. He had received the anonymous tip-off and headed straight here to get to the bottom of it. He was now wishing that he'd spent more time fact checking. "It gave details of your . . . er . . . *alleged* plans to

remove some of the Council as well as details of how Hunter defeated you."

Chromosome's face flushed with rage. Grutt instantly knew "defeated you" was the wrong thing to say when standing in front of one of the most merciless super-villains on the Council.

"I . . . I mean slipped through your fingers . . . "

That was no better.

Chromosome instantly understood who had sent that e-mail. In ordinary circumstances it would be nothing more than a prank. But the Council of Evil took every lead seriously. A number of spam e-mail companies had unexpectedly gone up in flames when the Council's e-mail address had found its way on to their servers.

"It looks like you have been misled, Grutt. The victim of a prank. Spam e-mail, nothing more."

Grutt nodded, suddenly eager to leave. Chromosome relaxed, and a smile found her lips.

"But no harm seems to have been done. Before you leave, tell me who else have you told? It would be embarrassing if other Council members got the wrong idea, wouldn't it?"

Ambassador Grutt sagged with relief as the tension in the room was dispelled. "I have told nobody, I assure you. I came straight here to see you."

"You did? Good."

The ambassador's own smile faltered. Her words had

somehow seemed very final. And he remembered that seeing Chromosome smile was never a good thing.

"I should be going."

He turned to leave but the patter of tiny feet made him look at the floor. The Legion surrounded him, the palm-sized spiders rearing on their back legs, chrome fangs clicking menacingly.

Chromosome took her seat, crossed her legs, and clasped her hands together to get comfortable. "I don't think so, Ambassador. Questioning my loyalty is not something I take lightly. Especially when you are correct."

The ambassador could only give a gasp before the Legion crawled all over his body like hot needles burning his flesh. He screamed and fell to his knees as tiny mouths bit into him. Within fifteen seconds his squeals had abruptly stopped and the Legion scattered back into the darkness, leaving nothing but a pile of broken bones wrapped in torn robes.

Chromosome had to think fast. She had to delete Ambassador Grutt's e-mails. Then she would strike back at Hunter by destroying his only chance of ever restoring his parents' memories.

She would kill Psych.

Jake thought he'd go crazy if he looked at one more Web page. He had decided to trawl deeper through

Villain.net and the Internet as a whole, to try to find a crumb of information on Psych. But he had found nothing.

He was getting restless, and that usually made him feel angry. He wanted to contact Mr. Grimm but had no number, no e-mail, *nothing*. Grimm was always the one to initiate contact. Jake was convinced he would have heard from him after the Statue of Liberty incident, but he didn't seem to be returning anytime soon.

Jake shook his head when he realized that he had been lazily watching multicolored sparks leap between his fingertips as his powers swirled inside him like bad indigestion. He had never seen energy spark from any other hero or villain, and wondered if it had something to do with the mutating powers in his body. And he found himself again regretting ever opening that spam e-mail from Villain.net. But it was too late to turn back time.

Feeling melancholy, Jake decided he'd go and visit his family again. Mr. Grimm had told him often enough that Jake was the prime target for any hero, villain, or Enforcer so he should keep a low profile. But right now Jake didn't care. He was going to do things *his* way.

Jake teleported into his old bedroom with a loud bang. He reasoned that since his family was conditioned not to see or hear him, then they wouldn't have heard the

The Race Begins

noise coming from upstairs. Plus, it got around the motion sensors outside.

He felt annoyed that his room was now being used as a dumping ground for any old bric-a-brac. He made his way downstairs, as loudly as he did when he lived there—but came to an abrupt halt halfway down. The hallway was decorated with bright tinsel and flashing Christmas lights arranged around the door. Even after destroying the Christmas tree in the shopping center, he'd forgotten what time of year it was—an easy thing to do within the drab gray walls of an empty Transylvanian castle.

He entered the living room. His mother had gone overboard with the decorations as usual. A bushy Christmas tree, too big for the room, had its top bent to follow the ceiling. It dominated the corner with enough lights to outshine Las Vegas.

Jake felt a lump in his throat. When he was younger, he and his sister always helped their parents decorate the tree. It was an exciting time, charged with the magic of the season. But as he got older and more cynical, he begged off such chores, and had long ago started taking for granted the effort his parents put into making the place look jolly.

He noticed a line of Christmas cards on the shelf and picked them up. His name was not on a single one. Not even from his grandmother.

Feeling utterly alone, Jake followed the sound of voices and headed into the kitchen. His family was gathered around the table eating. Beth was excitedly talking about her day at school. Their mom laughed in all the right places as she half-read the newspaper, and his dad nodded eagerly as he watched the news on the television.

Jake pulled up an empty seat. *His* seat. Nobody paid him the slightest attention. He waved a hand in front of Beth's face as she twittered on about her role in the school choir. She didn't react, even when he motioned to slap her, stopping less than an inch away.

Jake was nothing to them.

He reached over and snagged an overcooked sausage from his dad's plate. He didn't seem to notice the theft. Jake ate half of it, but found his appetite was gone. He didn't listen to their conversation, the words drifting over him like water. Just being with them was enough for him.

Old Jake would have moodily picked at his food before retreating to his bedroom or slinking outside to cause mayhem with Scuffer and the others.

That all seemed like a million years ago now.

When his phone suddenly vibrated in his pocket, he answered it without moving away from the table, shouting to hear himself over his family.

"Yeah?"

The Race Begins

"Hunter, this is Mr. Grimm. I . . . where are you? Who is talking in the background?"

Jake quickly stood and walked into the living room.

"That was the TV. You were right about Chromosome. She had no intention of helping me."

"I heard all about it. I'm sorry it turned out that way."

Jake found his next words difficult to say, especially after the last several weeks. "Thanks for watching out for me."

"To be forewarned is to be forearmed. I have some news of interest to you regarding Psych."

"You know where he is?" Jake's eyes shot around the room. The festive atmosphere made him want to be part of his family more than ever before.

"No. His team split up several years ago and he recently retired in secret."

"Retired?"

"We all grow old. And with fewer heroes around these days, many seek early retirement. Out of the limelight and gaining a longer life span because of it. I have checked the Foundation computers and there is no record of where he is now. He just surfaces every now and again to do some freelance work when he needs the money. I do not have time to help you fully, so you must take the next steps on your own. And hurry, as Chromosome will have her own methods of tracking

him, and I suspect after the beating you gave her that she will be looking to hurt you by killing him. That's one thing about the Council of Evil; they all tend to think alike."

"So what do I do?"

"Psych was part of a superhero team. I have an address for one of them. Blizzard. I'll text his details over now. Find him and you take a step in hunting down Psych. Good luck."

The line went dead before Jake could ask any further questions. Moments later a text message arrived. He had a destination: Turkey.

Manhunt

Chromosome walked quickly through the citadel corridors. The citadel dominated the central island, housing the Council chamber on the upper levels, with administration offices and accommodations below. Running an evil empire was big business, with profits in the billions. When the Council of Evil issued permits to allow villains to carry out their sinister plans, they took a diabolical percentage of the villains' ill-gotten gains. It was an endless process that required constant monitoring of which villains were successful, still alive, had the correct permits, and so on. For any villain who tried to cheat the system there was a severe penalty: death. It required a lot of administrative staff.

Chromosome was sure that Ambassador Grutt's absence wouldn't be noticed for several hours. Now she had to delete his personal computer records to remove all traces of Hunter's e-mail. She mentally kicked herself for killing him. It was one thing to dispatch a hero or wailing security guard, but murder of the Council's own staff was heavily discouraged and

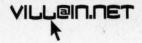

often led to detailed inquiries. Chromosome couldn't deal with that hassle right now.

Without the president and access to his military might, her goal of restarting the planet would have to wait a little longer. She had persuaded three other members of the Council to back her, but that had created problems. She obviously couldn't reveal her identity, so she used a code name to remain anonymous. The problem was that her coconspirators also had to use pseudonyms to conceal their identities. So she didn't know who *they* were either. It wasn't the best way to form a conspiracy.

She passed through the open-plan section of Grutt's domain. If you ignored the fact that the citadel looked like a crooked finger pointing skyward, and was located in an extinct volcano, run by the eight most notorious evil masterminds of the day, then the office block looked just like any other business. People chatted at the water cooler, workspaces were outfitted with advanced workstations that linked to a quantum-processor server (that was imbued with artificial intelligence, and was called "Ernie"). The walls were decked with personal decorations and there was even a Christmas tree in one corner.

Chromosome ignored the curious looks, and people swiftly stepped aside for her. It was rare for a Council member to come down here. She reached Grutt's private office and slipped inside.

Manhunt

It only took a few moments for her to delete the e-mail and wipe his computer's drive. Her Legion had already disposed of his bones in the ocean. Jagged cliffs surrounded the nine islands, so there was no beach for the evidence to wash up on. It was a simple crime. Now she could get on with the business of tracking down Psych.

Grutt had been a lesson to Chromosome not to be so impatient. If she held the hero hostage, she might yet be able to coerce Jake into assisting her hostile takeover.

Then she would kill Psych.

Jake took shelter under the trees on the university campus. It was a hot day. Sweat rolled from his brow and his skin itched like crazy. He had put on some sun-block, but still his photosensitive skin prickled.

Grimm had provided him with a picture and a location. The man formerly known as Blizzard was now tutoring at the Sisli Campus of Istanbul University, under his real name of Amr Munir. He was teaching trainee nurses, the job that he'd had before he began fighting crime around the world.

Jake was standing between the main building and the parking lot. He didn't want to risk approaching Munir in public, and he didn't want to cause a fight. His plan was straightforward. He would wait until Munir was

somewhere secluded and then he would ask for help in locating Psych.

It was the middle of the afternoon, and in the distance, Jake could hear the distinctive singsong voice calling Muslims to prayer. Munir walked from the building, circled the entrance fountain, and crossed through the lot toward his car. Jake hid behind some trees and watched him. Amr Munir was handsome and Turkish, in his mid-fifties with a fine head of gray hair, and deep brown skin with a bushy mustache. He wore a pale beige suit and held a briefcase, looking every bit the respected tutor. He held himself ramrod straight, but Jake noticed a limp, most likely an old war wound from his superhero days. He climbed into a black S-class Mercedes and pulled away.

Jake shot straight up in the clear blue sky. There was no cloud cover, but he knew if he climbed up just a few hundred feet a casual observer on the ground would think he was nothing more than a large bird. He followed Munir's car as he turned right at the gates and followed the circular route to get onto the main 0-1 highway that ran through this part of the city.

Jake paid close attention to which black car he was following. If he so much as glanced away he could end up following the wrong one. The three-lane highway was busy with commuter traffic and trucks. He trailed Munir eastward as he followed the road in a big U-turn and approached the more residential areas of the city. These sat on the banks of the Bosporus Straits, the wide body of water that cleaves Istanbul in half and actually separates the European and Asian continents. If Jake had recalled anything from geography, he would have known Istanbul is the only city in the world that sits on two continents. But at least he remembered they had a half-decent national soccer team.

Ahead, Jake could see the sun glinting on the wide stretch of water, and the highway continuing across the Straits on the Bosporus Suspension Bridge that links the continents. Talking to Munir in his car would be the most discreet place available.

The Mercedes rolled onto the bridge. Jake flew ahead and perched on top of the bridge's first tower, three hundred and fifty feet over the road, and waited for him to pass. As Munir drew near Jake launched himself straight down. His stomach lurched as he headed for the Mercedes's roof at high speed. At the very last moment he phased through the car and landed on the backseat with such force that the entire vehicle rocked.

Munir stared in the mirror, aghast. His car swerved across the three lanes and into the emergency lane in a clamor of car horns. Munir stamped on the brakes and the car skidded to a halt. Momentum slammed Jake's head against the back of the passenger seat.

"Who are you?" Munir demanded as he turned around.

"My name's Jake Hunter." Jake studied him to see if he recognized the name. There was no response. "I don't mean you any harm."

"Get out of my car!"

"I need your help, Blizzard." Again he looked at the man for a reaction, but there wasn't one. For a second Jake thought he had followed the wrong vehicle.

"My name is Amr Munir, and I ask you again to leave."

Munir wasn't reacting the way any normal person would if somebody phased through the roof of their moving car. His reaction told of years of experience with Supers.

"You used to be known as Blizzard, formerly a member of the Justice Federation before you went into retirement."

Munir locked eyes with Jake for a second. Then he suddenly lifted his hand and fired his superpower at Jake.

A feeble spray of snow issued from his hand like the last dribble of a spray can. It floated pathetically in the back of the car.

Munir shook his hand in frustration. "Darn it!"

"Take it easy! I just want to talk."

The Turk wasn't listening. He examined his fingertips with a look of sadness. "Fading so quickly now," he murmured. Then he looked at Jake, the defiance gone from his eyes. "Are you here to kill me?"

Manhunt

"I told you I just want to talk. Who would try and kill you anyway?"

"I made many enemies during my time with the JF. Villains carry heavy grudges."

"Tell me about it," Jake muttered. "And what's with your powers? Do they grow old too?"

"Alas, yes. That is why most of us volunteered to share them with the Hero Foundation. What I would do to have them back. . . It's a heavy loss to bear, like losing an old love." He looked dreamily away for a second, before scrutinizing Jake. "You are a Downloader?"

"Does it show?"

"Teleportation, flying, and phasing through my car roof. Yes it shows. Normally you would expect to fly, perhaps shoot ice from your fingers . . . and then have another, almost useless, power such as spoon bending. Downloaders are fortunate. They have a choice. So why did you seek me out?"

"I need to find your colleague Psych. Can you tell me where he is?"

"Why do you need *him*?" Jake heard the disapproval in Munir's voice.

"He wiped out my family's memories of me. They don't see or recognize me at all. I want them back."

Munir considered this for a moment.

"If I knew where he was, or even his real name, then he has no doubt wiped that from *my* mind. He was always a rebel, never listening to orders and running up huge gambling debts. I was glad to see the last of him."

"I thought you superteams were all good friends?"

Munir laughed loudly. "Ah, you're so young! No. That is what led to the disbanding of the Justice Federation. It was fun for a while, but we soon learned to dislike one another's habits. Small things led to big arguments. One time one of us accidentally burned down a whole apartment block because Psych used all the toilet paper!"

Jake smiled. He knew *that* feeling.

Munir continued. "But Psych, he was a problem. One step away from being a villain, in my mind. And which side are you on, I wonder?"

"My own."

Munir nodded, satisfied with the answer. "He caused waves with another member of our group, a very pretty girl who went by the name of the Hooded Harrier." He smiled at Jake expectantly, and then shook his head when it became clear the name meant nothing.

"Before your time. She was beautiful. Scottish and a fiery temperament to match. They had a *thing* for a while, but of course, like a lot of relationships with colleagues, tension rose. Arguments started and they split up. Overnight, that was the end of the Justice Federation. Defenders of world security, champions for the oppressed . . . disbanded because of a failed love affair."

Jake felt suddenly uneasy as Lorna popped into his mind.

"Would this 'Hooded Harrier' know where Psych is?"

Munir nodded. "I heard they kept in touch for a while; we all did. But most of us went our separate ways, retiring from superhero life and choosing more sedate careers."

"Can you tell me how to find her?"

"Your quest to find Psych means that much?"

"It means *everything* to me. That's all that's keeping me going right now."

Munir sized him up, and then closed his eyes, relenting. "Then I will tell you where to find her, Mr. Hunter. But don't expect the warmest of receptions from her."

"Tell me where to find the hero they call Psych."

A deep rumble answered the question, a sure sign that Ernie, the artificial intelligence, was thinking. A holographic display projected a large, constantly shifting blob. Ernie had originally been programmed with a human face, but his constant sarcastic expressions had driven everybody to distraction, so it was replaced with a sphere, which twisted and contorted according to how busy the system was. Ernie had already modified his own programming and added a color scheme to indicate how he felt about the tasks asked of him.

"There is no current record of his location on file."

Chromosome thought that might be the case. She looked around the empty chamber, with its walls padded with triangular noise suppressors so conversations could not be overheard. The room was designed as a secure access point to communicate with Ernie. There was no typing, no logs that could be traced, and nothing that could be hacked into like a conventional computer.

"Have you cross-referenced his name with any information on the Justice Federation?"

Ernie's color changed to a dull red, a sign of annoyance. "Of course I have, as well as pseudonyms, lists of villains he convicted, and school records. Not one of which assisted in tracking him down."

Chromosome scowled. She hated talking to Ernie; his tone reminded her of her first, and only, boyfriend. He'd been sarcastic too, right up until his last words. She didn't regret killing him, but would always remember him sneering, "*Yeah, right. As if you'd be able to stab me with that claw!*"

"Ernie, you are capable of quantum processing, analyzing data at incredible speeds and through *multiple* dimensions. Surely you can predict *where* he'd be?"

Ernie rumbled again as he digested the request, and

his color returned to neutral white, a sure sign he was computing the possibilities.

"It could be possible. But it will take a lot of processing power to compute a possible future. That is indeed an interesting task for a change."

Silence filled the chamber. Chromosome crossed her arms and impatiently drummed her fingers on her elbow. "Well? How long will it take?"

"If I take all nonessential systems off-line, then, maybe two days."

"We only have hours. Do what you have to."

Ernie ran everything on the islands: security systems, sea and air defenses, every computer terminal in the citadel, and everything else—including the vending machines.

"And, Ernie, if anybody asks, don't tell them what you are doing. This is a priority Council operation, Need to Know Only security. And I'm the only Council member who needs to know."

Taking almost every system off-line would raise a few eyebrows, but Chromosome was racing against time. She had to find Psych. Her plan depended on it.

Jake examined the printed map in his hand. The hard rain had made the ink run so that it was almost unreadable. Ever since he had arrived in Glasgow, Scottland, it had been raining from charcoal skies. He had flown around the city for several minutes before finally following the Clyde River southeast to a place called Rutherglen.

He landed in a bank of trees at the side of a railway track and walked out into a drab housing development. The burned-out car next to him told him everything he needed to know. Monotone four-story blocks of apartments surrounded Jake and made him feel hemmed in, reminding him of Diablo Island. Loud music and raised voices echoed eerily around the concrete canyons. The few Christmas decorations that were on display did nothing to cheer the place up.

Jake found the building he wanted and took the outdoor staircase, which smelled like a public toilet, walking up to the top floor. He looked around in dismay. This was the type of neighborhood that offered few chances for the people who lived here. He had always been a troublemaker, a bully destined to end up on the wrong side of the law, but he had been brought up as a privileged kid. And he was feeling ashamed for throwing it all away. No matter how bad this environment was, he knew most of the people who lived here would turn out better than him.

He reached a door with peeling blue paint and knocked. Jake heard a chain being unlatched, and then the door swung inward. Sandra Sinclair, aka the Hooded Harrier, stared at him. She was almost fifty, but looked much younger, even though she was wearing a fierce expression.

"Hi," Jake began before the woman sidestepped and he saw a wall of flesh racing down the narrow corridor. He heard a roar like an injured lion, caught glimpses of a blue jumpsuit and powerful shoulders scraping ruts in the narrow plaster walls. Jake focused on an enormous fist the size of a bowling ball—which connected with his face.

Jake was punched over the concrete balcony and sailed across the parking lot, before landing on a rusty van that crumpled like a pancake underneath him, windows exploding.

Although his ever-present force field had cushioned the blow, he still felt groggy. He looked up to see an impossibly huge figure spring down from the balcony. It was Scuffer. Jake had walked straight into a trap. Whether Munir had turned him in, or the Enforcers had just been lucky, he didn't know. But it served him right for letting even a retired hero live.

Scuffer effortlessly picked up a small car and swung it down on Jake. Jake flipped to one side, dropping to the tarmac just as Scuffer slammed the car onto the van.

Enforcers ran out of Sinclair's apartment, spreading out on the balcony with their guns trained on the action below. Jake swore at himself for being too careless. He tried to climb to his feet—but another pile-driving punch landed on him. The blow drove Jake one hundred feet backward, smashing through slender tree trunks that lined the embankment of the railway line. The wood splintered with each impact, the trees falling over with a loud crack.

Jake bounced across the railway tracks and rolled for some time before coming to a halt. His breathing was labored. He forced his eyes open. One was swollen. He saw that he was lying in between the tracks next to a railway station. There were only a couple of people on the long thin platform. One was so engrossed in his newspaper that he didn't even look up. Another was listening to an iPod and singing loudly, and badly, with his back to the action.

Scuffer pushed his way down the embankment, his great deformed head sweeping from side to side as he sniffed the air. The noise was disgusting, as if he had a nose full of mucus. He zeroed in on Jake and roared, one powerful fist pounding into his chest like a deranged gorilla. Jake thought that whatever the mutating power was that he'd cast on Scuffer, it had turned him into a killing machine, one powered not by the feeble intelligence his old friend had once had, but by pure animal instinct.

Scuffer menacingly approached Jake. Out of the corner of his eyes, Jake saw his chance. He lunged at the ogre, grabbing him around the throat and thrusting

Manhunt

Scuffer's head back—just as a commuter train shot past in the opposite direction, horn blaring.

Jake forced Scuffer's head against the rapidly moving wall of steel. The train windows shattered and metal buckled. For a second Jake hoped that Scuffer was going to collapse. Then the train passed and the brute effortlessly batted Jake away. The impact hadn't seemed to injure him at all.

Jake leaped to his feet and took a flying jump onto the station platform. Scuffer followed, leaping in one long bound. Jake heard Scuffer land behind him and turned—ducking as a fist wheeled round and shattered the station sign just above Jake's head.

Jake sprinted up the platform, between the two still-oblivious commuters. Scuffer followed like a charging elephant. Jake knew he could simply fly away; even Scuffer couldn't jump that high to follow him. But then he would be unable to talk to the Hooded Harrier. He had to get rid of Scuff and the Enforcers if he had any hope of tracking down Psych.

Scuffer was catching up. Jake flew forward, only a few feet from the ground, but fast enough to increase the distance between them and give himself time to think of a plan. To the north of the station was a rail yard with rows of rolling stock. All around the yard was an industrial complex, and reaching into the air, the steel beams of a huge construction project being built to the east.

Jake landed between rows of heavy iron open-topped hopper wagons that were filled with limestone. He had a moment to think. Scuffer possessed incredible strength, an acute tracking ability, and was able to leap large distances. Jake doubted he could win the battle of strength, and he obviously couldn't hide for long, so he had to make the most of his other powers. Jake winced as he felt his chest and eye regenerate. This was the first time he had ever been in a situation where he had to *outwit* the enemy. And the fact that it was Scuffer was just embarrassing.

The ominous crunch of gravel and gruff breathing signaled Scuffer had caught up with him. Jake knelt down and peered between the wheels of the wagons. He could see Scuffer's feet as he prowled on the opposite side of the freight wagon. Jake held his breath as Scuffer stopped. He could hear snuffling. Then he watched with relief as the feet walked directly away from him.

Jake wondered if he could pin Scuff down by toppling the wagons on him. Evidently Scuffer must have been having a similar thought. . . .

Jake heard rapid footfalls and instinctively shot into the air—just as Scuffer charged into the hopper wagon with a long running head start. The wagon clanged from the impact and jumped off the track. Tons of freight teetered for a second before toppling over. The cargo of limestone poured out across the track where Jake had been.

Jake hovered above the creature and unleashed an intense radioactive blast. The green wave rippled the air with its ferocity and knocked Scuffer off his feet. The heat was so intense that a section of the rail track he was standing on melted like chocolate.

Scuffer rolled backward, Jake continuing the onslaught until Scuffer smashed into a tube-shaped silver tanker filled with liquid petroleum gas. The radioactive heat detonated the load.

The orange fireball was blinding. An invisible shock wave blasted into Jake and sent him spinning through the air across the rail yard and into a line of flatbed trucks carrying shipping containers.

The explosion blew a crater in the middle of the yard and Jake could feel the heat singe his eyebrows as the fireball rose to the drab clouds like a mini-nuclear detonation.

For a few moments nothing stirred except the fragmented, burning remains of the tanker and the dull patter of rain. Black smoke covered the yard like dense fog.

Jake tried to climb to his feet but fell over—his leg was twisted completely the wrong way, a shard of bone poking out. He felt a jolt of pain but knew his superpowers were smothering the agony he really should be feeling. With a crack his leg twisted around of its own accord, and rapidly began to heal.

He had been surprised by the power of the blast; it was surely a giant killer. Then he noticed movement in the smoke and Jake's mouth fell slack. Scuffer was rising from the flames, his skin red-raw and covered in cuts. He pounded his chest and roared to the sky.

Jake was beginning to get a sinking feeling that his old pal Scuffer was indestructible. That would pose a *huge* problem.

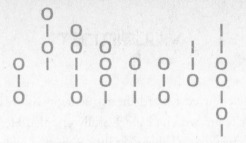

Final Destination

Technicians across the hangar were all talking at once as they tried to access the computer systems and internal phone lines. They were all getting a "system busy" message. Chromosome had entered the hangar with a few of the Legion in tow. It was a colossal space, housing the discus shuttles used by the Council. They were fast, undetectable by radar, and comfortable, ranging in size from private shuttles to large troop carriers containing mobile communication hubs—essentially a series of monitors and video cameras for each of the Council members so that they could talk to villains worldwide in the privacy of cyberspace without having to leave the island.

Chromosome preferred the smaller shuttles, like the one Hunter had destroyed on Liberty Island. But getting to one right now was proving difficult. Since Ernie had rerouted all processing power at her request, the entire island had become chaotic. Initially manual alarms had rung out to indicate they were under attack. When it became clear that Ernie had powered everything down, suspicion moved toward the rogue supervillain Basilisk and his team, who had successfully crippled Hero.com. Was he turning on Villain.net too? Repeated requests for Ernie to respond had revealed nothing.

It had taken a while for Chromosome to reach the hangar, as the corridors were full of staff running like worker ants. At one point she had seen Fallout looming through the corridor and she hid. He could well be one of her coconspirators, but without confirmation she didn't want to run into any other Council member who might delay her.

Chromosome walked quickly along the raised plat-form at the back of the hangar where the key trans-portation offices were located—Air Traffic Control and the Command Post, which was her destination.

Inside, the Command Post looked like most car ser-vice depots, with a counter bisecting the room and a bored-looking man sitting on a stool behind it. He looked nervous when Chromosome entered and put down his Playstation PSP as the Legion scurried to close the door behind her.

"Chromosome, ma'am. I was not expecting you here today."

"I need a shuttle." Chromosome thought back to the old days when being a villain was something you did for fun, working off your gut instincts. In those days there would be no problem jumping in the pilot seat of an aircraft and taking off. But with the current Council of Evil regulations there was so much *paperwork*.

"Uh, the computers are down at the moment."

"So? My business can't wait! Give me the ignition card." Like some modern cars, the shuttles could only operate if the pilot had the right ignition card, similar to a credit card, which unlocked the ship and started the engines.

The man licked his lips nervously. It was never good to argue with a Council member. But still, these were the Council's own rules.

"Do you have a B161 form?"

Chromosome laid both hands on the counter and leaned forward, smiling brightly. When she spoke her voice was seductive.

"I don't need those silly forms, do I?"

The man broke out in a sweat and he felt as if his brain was trying to seep out of his ears. He knew the rules, but the sweet melody of her voice convinced him everything was fine.

"N-no. Of course not."

"Then give me an ignition card for a shuttle."

The man half turned, then the nerdy clerk side of his brain kicked in and he frowned as he remembered something.

"But you already have one out . . . "

A flash of annoyance crossed Chromosome's face,

breaking the spell. Her persuasion powers only worked if she could keep a light-hearted tone, and right now she was feeling so stressed that she snapped.

"It was destroyed, you fool! That's why I want another! And, no, I refuse to fill out any of your ludicrous insurance forms again!" She had tried to report the shuttle loss through the Council's automated telephone system, but got lost when she pressed the wrong number on her phone's keypad. The phone system was evil incarnate.

The clerk had now fully recovered himself, and he crossed his arms defiantly.

"Then you know the rules, ma'am. I just—"

"Please! You must!" The charming voice was back, and the man was briefly reminded of his daughter asking for some present for Christmas. He smiled and patted Chromosome's hand without realizing what he was doing.

"Of course, don't worry. I'll sort it out."

He tapped a code into a safe under the counter and withdrew a small card, which he handed over to Chromosome. She snatched it, but he wouldn't let go.

"Now what's the magic word?" he said in a fatherly voice.

Chromosome was feeling too angry to keep up the pretense. She placed a finger on his lips to silence him.

"Thank you. You will tell nobody about this."

She removed her finger—and the man's smile

faltered as skin rapidly grew between his lips. It had the consistency of melted cheese, but the stringy flesh soon covered his mouth until he looked as though he'd been born without one. Then his nostrils sealed themselves too, and the man fell to the floor, suffocating as he clawed at his face.

Chromosome watched his struggle with interest, then remembered that she had to stop casually killing people like this. It would get her into trouble, and she didn't have time to dispose of this body like she had with Grutt. She quickly crossed the hangar to the shuttle, where she would wait until Ernie announced Psych's location.

What she wasn't aware of was that Grutt's remains had been found, and at that moment Necros was staring at the pile of bones and robes and coming to correct conclusions. . . .

Scuffer shattered the railway sleepers with a single punch as quickly as Jake could chuck the heavy concrete slabs. Scuffer's entire body looked both raw and, in patches, black from where he had been burned, but he showed no signs of pain. If anything it seemed to make him angrier. Jake had attempted to take to the air the moment he saw Scuffer was still alive—but instead he fell flat on his face.

His flying powers had deserted him once again.

Jake was shocked. Chromosome wasn't around to cancel them out, so he knew they must have permanently disappeared. As part of him was fused with Villain.net and his powers had been amplified, he had assumed that he no longer needed to download specific powers. The last few times he'd logged on to Villain.net, he had just downloaded from *any* icon he liked the look of. Now he remembered that he had only selected two, rather than his usual four powers, before leaving the castle. He was paying the consequences, and he just hoped nothing else ran out.

He'd been so engrossed with his thoughts he hadn't realized Scuffer was next to him until a mighty fist closed around his neck and pitched him into the steel cargo container. Luckily Jake's force field absorbed the damage.

Scuffer pressed his twisted face closer to Jake and loudly sniffed at him. Jake recoiled; Scuff smelled as if he'd been living in a sewer. As the grip tightened he was finding it difficult to breathe and he realized that Scuffer was trying to pull off his head.

"Scuff! It's me . . . Jake . . . ," he spluttered.

Scuffer seemed to relinquish his grip—but Jake's relief was brief. Scuffer yanked Jake away from the container, then repeatedly pounded him into the steel. With each impact Jake could feel his strength ebb as the metal crumpled around him.

Final Destination

"Scuff! Warren . . . Feddle! That's your name!"

Scuffer hesitated and pulled Jake closer for scrutiny. Overhead, a pair of Chinook helicopters appeared; the tail ramps opened and a squadron of Enforcers aimed their weapons out of the door.

"Scuff . . . we used to be friends. Remember?"

Scuff grunted. It could have meant *anything*, but Jake chose to interpret it as a sign of recognition.

"You don't want to hurt me, do you? Remember the fun we used to have?"

Scuffer's eyes narrowed, and Jake wondered if he'd suddenly triggered a bad memory—such as what Jake had done to him in Moscow after he'd tried to rob him.

Bellowing with rage, Scuffer tossed Jake overhead like a ball. Jake soared through the air, completely out of control. For a horrible second his vision was filled with twin whirling rotors as a Chinook banked into position—but Jake was traveling fast enough not to get caught in the rotors' suction.

Jake curved back to earth and crashed through a row of parked commuter trains that had been covered in graffiti. He soared through one window, across the car and out through the opposite side in a shower of glass. He landed hard across the steel tracks, and felt the cold metal of a rail press into the back of his neck. He suspected that his shield's strength was beginning to weaken, and he felt a little wobbly.

He silently berated himself for not being better prepared. He was so consumed with finding Psych that he had failed to take care of himself.

He looked up through bleary eyes to see Scuffer bound across the yard in a single leap. The ogre landed on the track next to Jake and roared savagely. Jake tried to move—but the entire weight of the mutant was suddenly on top of him. Scuffer pinned Jake's arms with his knees, then punched him repeatedly across the face. Jake felt a tooth knock loose. Another punch cracked his jaw—which he felt snap back into place, a fresh tooth pushing from his gums as he healed.

Jake tensed his body, but only had free movement with his legs. He kneed Scuffer in the small of the back, but it was like kicking a rhinoceros.

Then Jake felt his neck tingle and realized it was because the train track was vibrating. Scuffer punched him again, and now he was facing the right direction to see a train speeding toward them. It was probably slowing down as it passed through the rail yard, but it was still easily doing seventy miles an hour.

Jake tried to push Scuffer aside, but for some reason he felt heavier than anything Jake had lifted before, as if his entire body had become denser, and Jake could only lift Scuffer a few inches.

Scuffer cupped both his hands together to form a huge fist to mash Jake's head. With his hands pinned down, Jake had only one option left. He squinted his eyes and hoped that he had correctly recalled the icon he'd carelessly clicked on.

A beam of red energy shot from Jake's eyes—and hit Scuffer full in the face. The beast fell backward, giving Jake the opportunity to slip free and roll off the track. He jumped to his feet—just as four hundred and sixty-six tons of Pendolino train struck Scuffer right in front of him!

Jake had to fight for his balance to avoid being sucked toward the express. The train's brakes screeched in a shower of sparks as it attempted to stop. Jake saw flashes of startled faces peering from the windows at him as it passed.

Jake half expected to see limbs scattered across the tracks, but instead was astonished to find that the collision with the train had done nothing more than to throw Scuffer across the yard and into a row of boxcars.

"He's completely indestructible!" Jake exclaimed aloud.

He glanced up at the Enforcer helicopters circling like vultures. The soldiers had not fired a shot; they were enjoying the fight too much. The Chinooks were hovering *just* beyond the range of his powers.

Jake glanced at Scuffer as he climbed to his feet, shaking his head woozily. At least the express train had had *some* effect on him. Jake looked across at the construction site, and his own advice rattled through his mind. He had to *outthink* Scuffer.

Unable to fly, Jake had to resort to sprinting across the yard as fast as possible. He reached into his energy reserves and hoped he possessed some type of super-speed . . . but his luck had run out.

Scuffer saw him run and beat his chest. That gave Jake precious seconds to reach the fence separating the rail yard from the construction site. He fired his radioactive blast ahead of him as he ran, and jumped over the molten metal as it formed a puddle.

Luckily the construction site was empty. All types of machinery lay around it: bulldozers, JCBs, cranes, cement mixers. Port-O-Potties lined the edge of the site, built around a towering steel skeleton of red iron girders that stretched up, forming the core of a new ugly tower block.

A plan was forming in Jake's mind. He didn't like it at all, but it was the only thing he could think of.

Scuffer bounded into the yard with a howl. He picked up a dirty yellow dump truck with both hands and lobbed it overhead. Jake jumped aside. The truck smashed into the mud beside him and flipped less than an inch over his head before landing upside down, and providing cover between him and Scuffer.

Jake rolled behind the truck and slid into a drainage ditch. He scurried forward on his hands and knees, spitting out the foul brown water that splashed into his mouth.

Scuffer was puzzled that he couldn't see Jake. He lumbered over to the truck and lifted the machine, expecting to find his prey underneath the scoop. He flipped it back onto its wheels with a howl when he saw that Jake had escaped. Then he raised his nose to the air and sniffed hard, his head turning as he caught the scent. Jake was crawling out of the ditch on the other side of the site. He ran for the iron girders and started to climb the steel frame like a lizard.

Jake was thankful he hadn't lost his climbing ability. As he reached the fifth floor he glanced down to see Scuffer looking up at him and pacing back and forth as he decided whether or not to follow.

Jake laughed to himself. "You're as dumb as a dog, Scuff old pal."

Scuffer walked around the framework as Jake reached the tenth floor and edged across the narrow steel beams to the side of the structure opposite Scuffer.

From the top, Jake had a good view of Glasgow. The river and hills to the north, drab housing developments to the south. He waited for Scuffer to follow him around before he extended both hands and fired a supercharged radioactive blast to the ground . . . but what came out was a feeble splutter of energy.

"Aw, no!" wailed Jake. His old faithful power had

deserted him too. He screamed, annoyed with himself for having let his powers dwindle so much, especially after using them so heavily. It was one thing to wean himself off them, but a foolish mistake to walk into battle without *any* weapons.

Scuffer must have sensed Jake's anguish because he moved to the foot of the tower. Jake was fairly certain that Scuff didn't have the balance to climb all the way up. And he was right.

Scuffer grabbed a beam and started to shake it.

At first nothing happened. Then Jake felt the iron quiver under his feet, and after twenty seconds the entire tower was shaking as if it was caught in an earthquake.

Jake's feet slipped from the wet metal and he fell, latching an arm around a beam to save himself. His feet pedaled the air. His climbing power had just vanished.

Unable to fly and unsure if he still had a protective shield, he was certain the fall would kill him. Scuffer shook the tower as if he was trying to dislodge a cat from a tree. Jake felt his grip start to give on the slick steel. And then he fell—CLANG!—landing on his back across another cross girder two floors down. He winced from the pain, but luckily his shield was still working to some degree. Jake rolled onto his chest and gripped the girder with his arms and legs. He didn't suffer from vertigo when he flew, but now that he only had one direction to go—down—he was *terrified*.

Final Destination

The sound of wrenching steel made him look up. The vibrations had started to loosen bolts. With a ping, steel bolts came free and a heavy girder plummeted down. Jake closed his eyes, his teeth rattling as the falling girder smashed against the one that he was clinging to before bouncing off several others and crunching against the concrete floor.

He watched as another girder ricocheted from the tower with a clang and smashed into the Port-O-Potties, squashing them flat.

All around Jake, girders began to collapse and plunge to earth. One barely missed whacking Scuffer across the head. Jake was trapped in a life-size game of Jenga.

Jake renewed his grip with one arm and extended the other. He just had to hope all his powers hadn't expired. He concentrated and shot an enormous fireball straight to the ground in between Scuffer and a line of construction vehicles. It was a wide shot, and left nothing but a deep impact crater that rapidly filled with water. But the force was enough to throw Scuffer away from the collapsing tower.

Startled, Jake lost his balance and fell.

His arms thrashed as he tried to latch on to something, but he rebounded like a pinball as he fell eight stories into the concrete foundations. Seconds later a pair of girders smashed down on either side of him before bouncing like poles and landing in the mud.

Jake groaned. One of his arms was broken, but the rest of him was in relatively good shape. He could teleport to safety, but where would that get him? He'd have to return at some point to get the information he needed.

Jake knew he had to fight this one to the end.

Scuffer pounced on him before he could stand. Jake's leg felt as if it was being plucked from its socket as Scuffer lifted him by the limb, then tossed him across the building site.

Jake smashed into the side of an empty cement mixer. He slid to the ground, winded. He watched, mesmerized, as the entire shaking tower collapsed in a thunder of metal, kicking up a cloud of dust that blotted out the ever-present Chinooks.

By throwing him, Scuffer had unwittingly saved Jake's life. The brute was flat on the ground and several girders bounced off him, but with no apparent harm.

Jake shook his head. "Unbelievable."

As soon as Scuffer got to his feet and strode through the crater caused by Jake's blast, Jake shot a fireball against the tail of the dump truck beside him—then leaped for cover under the cement mixer as thirty-eight tons of gravel cascaded from the back of the truck and filled the crater, crushing Scuffer. As the last piece of gravel settled, a dusty gray cloud rose across the suddenly silent construction site.

Final Destination

Jake ran for the tree cover at the edge of the yard. The rain would dispel the cloud soon enough, but it would take some time for the patrolling Enforcers to realize that Jake was not buried beneath the destruction. He didn't for a moment think that Scuffer was dead under all that weight, but he hoped that he couldn't break out.

All Jake had to do now was get back to the woman in the apartment, and somehow persuade her to tell him what he wanted.

Chromosome sat quietly in the shuttle's pilot seat. In her youth in South Africa she had flown small Cessna planes, which had given her enough grounding to easily take control of these sophisticated machines, although she was too lazy to do so and always relied on the autopilot now. An alarm rang over the base and she frowned.

"Seal the island," instructed a voice over the PA system.

Chromosome started to feel a little worried as the reinforced hangar doors rolled closed in front of her. She would have to open them if she intended to fly out of the hangar.

Then the siren stopped and a new voice came over the PA, so cold and lifeless it made the citadel's staff shiver: Necros.

"We have a murderer among us. A slaughterer of our own kin. Ambassador Grutt has been murdered."

Chromosome could see the reactions across the hangar, mostly shrugs of indifference, as Grutt was not a well-liked man. But, surprisingly, murder on the island was something new.

"All Council members must return to the chamber for an emergency session. Anyone who doesn't will be deemed a *traitor*."

Chromosome sighed. She knew that she'd been caught. Still, she did not fear Necros too much; after all, she was planning to overthrow him. But the entire Council together would pose a problem and she still wasn't certain who her coconspirators were.

Through the craft's panoramic windows she saw somebody enter the Command Post—and run out seconds later screaming. Another body had been found. Chromosome rolled her eyes; she was just too kill-happy at times. Now it looked as if she would have to slay everybody in the hangar just to keep the discovery secret.

Then she noticed that people were pointing at her from the balcony area. They had obviously connected the dots. She rose from her seat—but it was too late, a female technician already had a radio to her mouth. Seconds later Necros's voice came over the PA.

Final Destination

"So, Chromosome. I never thought you had it in you."

The hangar lights flickered, causing the technicians to flee. They knew what was coming next. Chromosome stabbed the control button that sealed the ship's doors and sank back into the seat.

"Come on, Ernie . . . ," she whispered.

She strapped the harness tightly across her just as the hangar plunged into darkness; only the red emergency lights hinted at shapes and obstacles. The technicians who hadn't fled the hangar now cowered in the corners as Necros emerged. His voice echoed uncommonly loud across the hangar.

"Chromosome, I know you're here. I can smell your fear."

She held her breath as Necros's head scanned the hangar. She could just make out the rusted helmet that crowned his head, and the rotting cape that hung from his shoulders and trailed behind him. He walked past the shuttle, oblivious to her.

"I will find you." The sibilant voice sounded as if it was close to her ear. "I will make you suffer to show others that dissent among the Council will not be tolerated."

Chromosome smiled to herself. If only he knew that half the Council was ready to rebel against him.

"I suspected betrayal from the inner sanctum. Did you think I was foolish enough not to flush out conspiracies from my empire?" So that was how Necros saw the Council of Evil? His own *personal* empire?

Necros started circling the shuttle fleet, stooping to glance underneath the craft. "Of course, you will be expecting your coconspirators to come rushing in to save you. Because what better time to take me out than now? But I have to tell you, that is not likely to happen." Necros laughed, which sounded more like tortured souls wailing. "That is because you have *no* coconspirators, Chromosome. They were waiting to betray you."

Chromosome's pulse quickened as anger flared inside her. Surely he was just playing for time and making this up to provoke her.

"Nameless conspirators who could trust nobody to reveal their identities to . . . except perhaps the one person they were supposed to be assassinating. Oh yes, they came to me. All on their own, not knowing who else among the Council to trust. Knowing who the conspirators were, I could focus my suspicions on those who *had not* stepped forward."

Chromosome gripped the flight stick. She wanted to scream. And then she wanted to kill those who had betrayed her. They had planned to double-cross her—expose her at the crucial point so that *she* would be the one killed. The devious coconspirators had found a way to eliminate one of their own, which would curry favor with Necros and ensure their position in the Council. No doubt those who were in on the conspiracy were being paid substantial amounts of cash by wannabe Council members. Cash for honor, an old staple throughout history.

But now, that meant the Council of Evil would turn against Chromosome. In this time of escalating war against the Hero Foundation, they would have to crush anyone threatening to topple them. Alone, she was no match for the seven other powerful Council members. But. . . with Hunter by her side, there would be no stopping her.

Her cell phone, no bigger than a watch face, vibrated on her belt. She glanced at the message and finally found something to smile about.

Ernie had predicted Psych's location.

Using the Council shuttle would be pointless now as they could easily track her. Instead she teleported out of the hangar.

Jake was out of breath by the time he had climbed up all the steps of the tower block. He stopped close to the top and collected himself. His hands were trembling uncontrollably, and he knew that he needed to plug into Villain.net to recharge or he would collapse. He had sneaked back across the railway line, making sure he wasn't spotted by the Enforcer patrols that

were combing the construction site searching for both him and Scuffer.

Jake walked out onto the balcony and approached the open front door. He could hear voices in the apartment and raised his hand as he stepped inside.

Sandra Sinclair was standing in the living room beyond the door, chatting to an Enforcer who had a mug of coffee in his hand. He looked surprised as Jake threw a fireball straight at him. It was only small, that was all Jake had left, but it hit the coffee mug. The Enforcer fell, knocked out by the small explosion that slammed the mug against his head.

The woman gasped and backed away—falling onto her sofa, arms raised and a look of terror across her face.

"Please! Don't kill me! They showed up first!"

Jake had nothing left. He was seriously worried he wouldn't be able to teleport back to his lair. If Sinclair threw a pillow at him right now, he would probably fall to the floor. Jake recalled the skills he had amassed as a bully; fear and intimidation were art forms.

"Don't make me mad. You really won't like me when I'm mad."

"W-what do you want?"

"If you want to live, tell me where I can find your old boyfriend. Tell me where Psych is."

Sinclair's eyes looked frantically around, and what little color she had in her cheeks vanished completely.

Final Destination

"I don't know! It's been a few years since we last talked!"

Jake felt his stomach clench. He had been robbed of his final destination.

Psych was still beyond his reach.

0
1
1
0
1
0
0
0
0
1
1
0
0
1
0
1
0
1
1
0
0
1
0
0
1
1
0
1
1

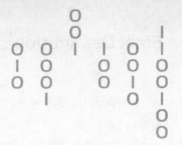

Expect the Unexpected

Jake was slumped on the massive four-poster bed in his new home. He had managed to teleport back to the castle. Appearing in the tower, he collapsed in front of the televisions.

When he woke, he found that Igor had carried him to the bedroom and plugged him into Villain.net. The genetically modified superpowers pumped through his system and revived him.

The television was playing endless news programs, all reporting on how major cities across the world had deployed their military in an attempt to stop the terrorist attacks—in reality a superhuman crime spree. He noticed that even the news reporters were referring to villains' names, but claiming that they were names of gangs.

He watched shaky news camera footage of a blazing dockland in Chicago. A single figure, who Jake knew from trolling Villain.net was named Wildfire, was hurling tongues of flame to incinerate the buildings. Reporters claimed that he was using a flamethrower. Since that was more believable than the fact that he was clearly throwing fire from his fingers, the public seemed to be swallowing it. The same was true of the "gang" attacks in Paris. The television showed footage of villains clinging to the side of the Eiffel Tower, having obviously flown there. The reporters stressed that thugs had climbed the tower, and the camera cut the moment the villains launched themselves off. Obviously the press were now in on the global conspiracy of super-silence. When he saw out-of-focus camera footage of the Statue of Liberty toppling over he closed his eyes.

He thought about Sandra Sinclair, the Hooded Harrier. He had managed to instill fear in her, and it had made him feel awful. How had he ever enjoyed being a bully? Seeing the older woman cower in terror had made him feel like a coward. He had tried to relax slightly and tried to be more friendly and reassuring. But the damage had been done. If Sinclair had any powers left she did not display them—she was just a scared ex-hero.

Jake had noticed that the apartment was filled with photographs of the Justice Federation. The Hooded Harrier had been very attractive back then, with long flame-red hair and a confident smile. Jake's eyes had bored into the picture of Psych.

Quivering with fear, Sinclair admitted she and Psych had remained pen pals for a while, but that had petered out. The only assistance she could give him was that Psych had moved to Australia. In his last letter, he mentioned opening a bar there.

Now, Jake climbed out of bed and paced around the empty castle. It was dark outside, and the snow piled against the window did little to raise his spirits. He stared at the crystalline statue of Chameleon.

"This is all your fault!"

He punched the frozen hero in frustration. The statue rocked, tilting at an angle against the wall. He raised a fist to strike the statue again but faltered. It was achieving nothing.

Australia. Jake knew it was a huge place. Finding out that Psych was there hadn't made his quest any easier.

Igor entered the room, rapping hard on the door for attention. Jake's rumbling stomach expected to see food, but Igor was empty-handed.

"What is it?"

Jake suddenly remembered that his butler was mute, so he gestured with his hands. Then he stopped and silently berated himself—he was *mute* not *deaf*. He waited patiently as Igor crossed over to the huge television screen that dominated the room and selected a channel. Jake was surprised to see that it was broadcasting the Presidential Shield.

Expect the Unexpected

Then the image changed to that of the president sitting behind his desk in the Oval Office. He talked straight to the camera.

"This is a message for the one they call the Hunter, broadcast on a secure channel. Even though we're unsure of your location, I'm certain this will find its way to you. We are living in an ever-shifting world. Friends become enemies. Enemies become friends. By kidnapping me you declared war on the United States, and that is not something I look lightly upon." The president shifted in his seat and cast a glance at a photograph of his family on the desk. "But you then had a change of heart and went on to save my life— from a danger that you placed me in, admittedly, but you voluntarily chose to reunite me and my team with our families. I know the pain you are feeling now, Hunter, the sense of loss. That is why I am granting you a presidential favor. At the end of this transmission is a data file. It contains the combined resources of the CIA and NSA—everything you need to find Psych."

The president smiled. "We *normals* do have access to information beyond what the Council and Foundation have. I trust your intentions remain honorable and you do not intend to harm him. You have my word that there will be no Enforcers or heroes waiting to trap you. Please know—I do this to return the favor you granted me. But after this is over you remain an enemy of both this country . . . and me. Consider this a temporary suspension in hostilities."

The image faded and was replaced with a rapid burst of high-pitched noises and rapidly flashing images that the castle's computers immediately translated into surveillance photographs, maps, and addresses.

Jake felt a wave of elation. This unexpected twist of fate was everything he needed. He was going to find Psych!

Jake inhaled deeply as he appeared among a knot of trees in Hyde Park, Sydney, Australia. He had always dreamed of having a beach house here and felt oddly closer to realizing his ambitions, although that was probably because he was close to finding Psych. The files had told him that the hero was now using his real name of Fred Hardcastle.

It was a warm summer day, and the heat made Jake's skin tingle, although Igor had applied sunblock. The problem with his photosensitive skin was something he would have to address before he moved here. He chased the thought from his mind, though—he was here to find Psych.

Jake left the park on foot and crossed the busy Macquarie Street as he headed into the financial district of the city. Huge skyscrapers loomed above him, looking modern and sleek. Here the streets were in almost permanent shadow and he felt relaxed as he followed the map in his hand.

Psych owned a bar located in the maze of skyscrapers that catered to executives and business types. Jake stopped at a street corner and stared at the luxury glass facade of the aptly named "Justice Bar."

He started to cross the street, but stopped as his phone rang. It was Lorna. Jake hesitated; he wanted to answer but the excitement of finishing his quest was too much. He ignored it and crossed over—just as the entire front of the bar exploded in a black cloud and a lethal hail of glass. Jake's head spun in confusion as glass showered around him, bouncing off his fully energized shield.

Then he saw Psych. He was lying in the middle of the street, cut and bruised as flames shot from his bar. Other than that, he hadn't changed much from Sinclair's photographs. Cars skidded around him—but an approaching bus, swerving around a chunk of flaming wreckage, headed directly for him.

Jake jumped between the bus and Psych and held up his hands. The bus skidded sideways toward him and he could see the panicked faces of its passengers—then it suddenly stopped as it ran into Jake's invisible shield, robbed of its momentum inches from flattening him.

He ran over to Psych and helped him up.

"Are you okay?"

The man's wide eyes swiveled from Jake to his ruined bar—just as Chromosome stepped out from the smoke. She registered surprise when she saw Jake, but she quickly recovered.

"Come to see your little friend die? How sweet." The words were as cold as steel, and as she spoke her Legion scurried forward.

Jake stepped in front of Psych and fired dozens of tennis-ball-sized fireballs into the crawling mass. The Legion split, avoiding the shots. Jake backed away as they surrounded him.

"We have already established that you can't defeat me," said Chromosome with a smile. "But I'm so sentimental that I will offer you a deal."

"I'm not bargaining with you," Jake spat out. He flamed two of the Legion that had raced forward with slender scorpion tails waving. The pseudo-creatures were flipped onto their backs, legs pumping as they burned.

"Dear Hunter, always so headstrong. Perhaps by working together we can both get what we want?"

"You double-crossed me once. Never again."

Jake lunged forward as though he were pushing an invisible wall. The air buckled as a telekinetic blast pounded into Chromosome, hurling her back into the blazing bar.

Expect the Unexpected

Jake grabbed Psych's arm and forced him to run as the Legion darted in pursuit.

"Can you fly?"

Psych hesitated before answering. "Yes . . . just a little bit though."

"Up!" Jake commanded. They soared into the air together, Psych lagging behind as they banked between skyscrapers. Jake zigzagged through the smoked glass avenues as they gained altitude. He couldn't see Chromosome following, and he noticed that Psych was struggling.

Jake doubled back and helped him land on the roof edge of a diamond-shaped building. From here they had a clear view northward across the wide harbor. The famous Sydney Harbour Bridge was to the left, the sail-like domes of the Opera House to the right. He noticed that a military tank sat next to the Opera House and several armed soldiers patrolled among the crowds of tourists. Jake remembered that every country was on high alert with the growing disturbances, and since the Statue of Liberty had been destroyed, the Australians were obviously protecting their national icons.

Psych was struggling for his breath. "That chook's a bit of a nutter! Who is she?"

Jake deciphered the Aussie slang. "Chromosome, from the Council of Evil. And she wants to kill you."

"Jeez, mate. Why? I'm retired."

Jake resisted the urge to shout at the hero for wiping his family's minds. Though he *had* done it on the orders of Chameleon . . . plus he was the only one who could bring them back to him.

"You still have your powers though. You can fly and wipe people's minds?"

"Yeah, but they're fadin' away with each birthday. I can't fly around much. I have problems goin' to the dunny, never mind swoopin' over the city!"

Jake got the gist of the conversation. "You're going to have to push yourself to fly. I can teleport us out of here but not right away. My power has to recharge."

"Watch out!" Psych yelled as Chromosome soared into view on her massive bat wings. She had not fully transformed to her monstrous visage, so she now resembled a twisted angel. Her Legion had evolved wings and swarmed around her like flies. They dive-bombed in, tails jabbing into Jake's back as he shielded Psych from the blows.

"Go!" yelled Jake, and he pushed Psych off the edge of the roof.

Jake swooped out over the busy ferry terminal. When he looked back he saw that Psych was plummeting to earth. Chromosome had spiraled around to intercept the old hero. Then he remembered that she could dampen powers, like she'd done to his flying ability on Liberty Island. It wouldn't have taken much to strip Psych of his aging talent.

Jake rocketed forward.

The busy concourse below the building was full of people, many sitting in the sun enjoying a drink. Somebody saw the commotion above and screamed— it looked like something out of a nightmare as a winged creature swooped down on a falling man.

Chromosome stretched out and grabbed Psych's foot—five floors before he splattered on the ground—as Jake tackled him from the side. He was traveling so fast that they both cannoned through an adjacent set of plate-glass office windows, plowing through office desks, filing cabinets, and thinly partitioned walls before coming to a halt in a rain of paper. Office workers screamed and ran for cover, adding to the confusion.

Chromosome appeared at the window, her wings beating quickly to keep her hovering. The whimpers from Psych meant he was still alive. Jake sprang to his feet and swept a hand toward Chromosome. His telekinetic power lifted a copy machine and hurled it at her. She dodged aside as it spun past her—but wasn't quick enough to avoid a metal filing cabinet that struck her head, momentarily stunning her.

Jake shouted at Psych. "On your feet!"

He hauled the man around the edge of the office as the Legion flew in pursuit, like homing darts. Jake and

Psych crouch-ran through an aisle of cubicles as the Legion buzzed around, searching every nook.

A woman suddenly screamed as the Legion found her cowering under a desk. She sprinted away, the bugs ignoring her.

Jake pulled the older man under the cover of a desk, where they remained motionless as the Legion flew overhead before landing farther down the aisle. The mass of shifting creatures suddenly fused together with a sucking noise, forming one long featureless snake that silently slithered around the legs of desks. Its blunt head shot up as though listening.

Jake held his breath. He had wanted to find Psych without resorting to combat. Luckily the Legion headed away from him and the leathery sound of wings indicated Chromosome was still hovering at the window behind them. Jake looked down the cubicle rows ahead of him. They ended at a panoramic window.

The silence was shattered when Jake's phone suddenly rang. He knew without looking that it was Lorna.

His hand thumped the phone silent, but the damage was done. The Legion twisted around and whizzed toward Jake's hiding place.

"Run!" he yelled as he pulled Psych from under the table. They raced toward the window, Jake throwing a fireball to blow the glass out.

"I can't fly anymore!" wailed Psych. He felt Jake's

arm around his waist, and the next second they leaped back outside.

Jake took Psych's weight, but couldn't gain altitude because the man was too heavy. It was as though they were descending on an invisible zip line as they soared over the busy ferry terminal. Psych's legs kicked uselessly, narrowly clearing the smoking funnel of a berthed cruise liner. They sailed over the water and in between a hotel and an apartment block before landing and rolling on the dry grass of a park.

Jake got to his feet—unaware that Chromosome had soared after them. She fiercely booted him in the back, sending him sprawling, as she landed.

"I'm not playing games, Hunter! You help me or he dies *now*!"

The Legion, no longer a snake but still just as deadly, swarmed all over Psych. Articulated tails pinned his arms and legs to the ground, while others quivered over his face, ready to strike.

"By my side you can have *everything*, Hunter. You have untapped potential and I know how to use that. This is your last chance."

Jake looked between Chromosome and Psych. The Legion tightened their hold on him with a sickening crunch. Jake sighed, and then lowered his guard, defeated.

"Okay. You win. Let him go."

Chromosome squinted suspiciously at him. She had been expecting more of a fight. "Really? Just like that?"

Jake matched her gaze. Then he smiled. Chromosome was taken aback. It wasn't the innocent smile of a friend or coconspirator. It was the calculating look of a predator.

Jake raised his hand toward Psych. It felt as though his fingers were being pulled from their sockets, although physically they didn't change. He felt a new power charge through his system.

Before leaving, Jake had prepared himself. No longer would he walk blindly into battle. He had spent time selecting what he hoped were the right powers for just this situation.

The chrome bodies of the Legion began to stretch toward Jake as if he'd activated a giant vacuum cleaner. Their legs scrambled for purchase on Psych but they were losing grip. Jake had chosen a magnetic power to combat the living metal Legion. The creatures shook violently before relinquishing their grip on the man, and sprang toward Jake's hand. As they approached, Jake reversed the immense magnetic energy he was producing—the sudden polarity change ripped the Legion apart in a shower of atomized metal and green gloop.

Chromosome screamed and lunged for Jake. "No!"

Jake was ready for that. His other hand issued an

intense radioactive beam with such force that Chromosome was pitched head over heels.

Jake pulled Psych up by the wrist. The man rubbed his throat, trying to get his breath back.

"Mate! Thank God there're still heroes like you around!"

Jake's smile faltered, he didn't have the heart to correct him. "Yeah. Right, come on. We'll get away from here soon."

They ran away from Chromosome, who was screaming in pain as she clawed at the radioactive burns across her chest.

Jake hopped over a small fence as they ran from the park and took stock of his surroundings. Ahead were the massive white curves of the Sydney Opera House. Crowds of tourists stood around the magnificent structure, but their attention was firmly on the park where they had just seen a winged monster land.

The Australian soldiers took cautious steps forward, guns raised. Jake noticed that the barrel of the tank had swiveled around toward the park.

A British tourist grabbed Jake's arm as he ran toward them. He was excited, trembling hands holding a video camera.

"Did you see that? What landed in there?"

"You don't want to know," said Jake.

He then watched in amazement as the man ran

toward the park. An inhuman howl echoed from the trees—and Chromosome emerged, mutated and angry. She had transformed into the massive ogre that had nearly defeated Jake in America. One wing was still burned and hung limply, dragging across the ground. Chromosome was unable to adapt the injured limb into something useful.

The mass of tourists screamed as the villain lumbered from the trees like a prehistoric giant.

The soldiers opened fire. Bullets thudded into Chromosome but did nothing more than irritate her. She charged forward and slapped one man off his feet, then backhanded another.

The tank fired, rocking on its tracks. The missile blew up the flagstones under Chromosome's feet and smoke obscured the view. Jake heard the footsteps before he saw Chromosome running out of the smoke.

The terrified tank commander poked his head from the turret just as Chromosome reached the vehicle. She picked it up without effort and hurled it out into the bay. It smashed onto the deck of a ferry; the entire boat listed dangerously before righting itself.

Psych pushed Jake forward. "Go on, mate. Kill 'er!"

Jake stared at him. "Are you crazy?"

"I can't do it! Too old. Go on!"

Jake shook his head. He could feel his teleportation powers were almost ready. He just had to hold out for a minute longer. He grabbed Psych around the shoulders and took flight.

More tourists screamed and ran when they saw the flying boy. Chromosome charged toward the Opera House, people scattering in her wake.

Jake struggled to make it to the top of the tallest of the three curved concrete shells before his flying power refused to be pushed any further. He landed on the spine and clung to the side of the building, more than two hundred feet up.

"Why's this happened to me?" moaned Psych.

Jake strengthened his grip on the man. "Because you stole my family's memories of me! I want them back!"

"I didn't do anythin' to you . . . " He trailed off, his eyes growing as big as saucers. "Aw, no way! You're Jake Hunter, aren't you? Mate, I couldn't 'elp it. Don't kill me. It was Chameleon. Said he had a job for me! I only check in now an' again to get some extra wonga. I don't ask questions! Please . . . I don't wanna die!"

"Shut up! Can't you see I'm trying to save your life? I just want you to help me. Then you go free."

Psych nodded. "I like that, mate. Sounds like a perfect plan. I can get 'em back for ya—"

Chromosome's howl made them both look down. She was climbing the curved shell, taloned fingers and feet shattering the tiles as she heaved herself upward. Her ugly mouth hissed at them.

"Nowhere to run, Hunter! I just took your flight!"

He didn't even have to try the superpower to know that she was right.

Psych pulled something from his wrist and shoved it into Jake's hand.

"What is it?"

"A keepsake, mate. Y'know, just in case."

"Nothing's going to happen to you. Grab hold of me."

Psych strengthened his grip around Jake's waist. Pressing their backs against the dome, they shuffled higher. But the man's additional weight wasn't allowing Jake to move and his feet began to slip across the surface. They both slid slowly toward the advancing monster. Jake was holding Psych, so he couldn't use his hands to shoot at Chromosome. He squinted, hoping he still possessed the laser eyesight . . . but that had gone. Despite all his superpowers, he was yet again completely defenseless.

With the danger slightly out of reach, the crowds gathered below, watching the bizarre spectacle of the giant Chromosome gouging a path toward Jake and Psych.

"Get us outta here!" shouted Psych.

"I can't yet! Can you do something?"

"I'm all out!"

Jake tightened his grip on Psych and freed his left hand. A radioactive surge coiled out and fell wide, leaving an ugly black scar down the side of the shell.

Expect the Unexpected

"Mate! Are ya blind?"

"Shut up!"

Jake fired again. The tiles under Chromosome exploded, forcing her to jump aside. She landed awkwardly and slipped down the steep slope—but her claws ripped deep into the concrete and halted her fall.

Jake could feel Psych slipping and had to refresh his grip. He could feel his teleportation power rippling through his body like pleasant pins and needles.

"We're out of here!"

But before he could do anything else, Chromosome sprang up the shell, smashing into the concrete next to Jake. The tiles around him shattered from the impact, and he found he was no longer firmly attached to the building, but to hundreds of shattered tile fragments.

He fell.

Chromosome lashed out and plucked Psych by his shirt from Jake's grip just as Jake reattached himself to the dome.

Psych's shirt suddenly ripped in Chromosome's taloned fingers and he fell past Jake, bouncing off the shell.

"Psych!"

Jake threw himself forward and began sliding head-first down the slope, but he knew that without flight there was no way of reaching the man in time. Jake watched in horror as Psych slammed awkwardly onto the angled sloping roof. Even from this height he could see the way his neck was contorted as his body fell down the white tiles. Psych tumbled sideways before dropping among the crowd, which rapidly parted with further screams.

Jake laid his palms flat against the shell to arrest his own descent. He could feel the pain from friction burns as he came to a halt, hanging upside down. He blinked in shock. It wasn't the fact he'd just seen a man plummet to his death—it was the fact that it was the same man who had wiped the memories of his family.

And the one man who could restore them.

His only hope had just died. His quest had failed.

He heard cackling laughter from above. Chromosome had seen it all. Rage and anger made every muscle in Jake's body tense, but common sense trickled through his thoughts of revenge. Chromosome was somebody he couldn't defeat.

For the first time in his life, Jake chose to turn away from a fight.

He teleported from Sydney, leaving his hopes and dreams smashed.

Jake stared at the flames in the fireplace and resisted the urge to throw the frozen Chameleon onto the fire as he replayed the last few hours in his mind.

Expect the Unexpected

Jake had been thinking about his family at the moment he teleported—and had appeared in the middle of the living room where his family sat watching a movie.

Weak and upset, Jake had dropped onto a chair, his head in his hands, fighting tears of despair as they laughed at the film. Without Psych everything was lost.

He toyed with the object Psych had given him. At first glance it looked like a watch, and Jake wondered why the hero's last act was to pass it on. He wiped his bloodshot eyes and took a closer look. The watch face was a small glass bubble that held a turquoise liquid. Jake held it up to the light. The liquid moved by itself, silver particles glittering within. Then he noticed an engraving on the glass.

The words: Hero Foundation Sample Receptacle.

Jake's heart skipped a beat as he realized what he was actually looking at. He flipped it over. Underneath was a series of small needles that would prick the skin when the "watch" was worn.

Psych had given Jake a chance. Psych had donated his power—the ability not just to remove and restore memories, but to completely rewire brains, the manifestation of which was the turquoise liquid.

Jake was shaking, both from nerves and lack of power, as he fastened the device to his wrist. There was one button on the side of the bubble. Jake pushed it.

With a faint click the needles punctured his arm, but

he didn't feel anything. Then the liquid suddenly injected into his system with a hiss.

Jake had expected the usual feeling of strength that he got when downloading superpowers, but instead he felt ill. He took a deep breath, but the sensation just got worse.

"Come on!" Jake shouted to himself. He was so close to victory that he couldn't afford to be weak now. He stood on trembling legs between his parents and touched their heads. It was an unpleasant feeling, as if his fingers were actually sliding through their skulls directly into their brains.

"Remember me! Come on! I'm here!"

He was expecting a wave of energy, a flash of colors . . . *something* to happen. Instead both his parents suddenly looked unfocused, and sagged in their chairs.

"I'm here! It's Jake. Your son, Jake! Remember?"

Then they both started to convulse as if they were being electrocuted. Jake snatched his hands away, afraid that he'd hurt them. They shook for several more seconds before falling limp once more.

"Mom? Dad?"

He moved to Beth, who was watching her parents with a puzzled expression as her brain tried to work out exactly what was happening to them. Jake pressed his hand firmly on her head. She jerked as the last of Psych's power flowed through him.

Expect the Unexpected

"Beth? Can you see me?"

She drooled slightly. For a moment Jake thought he'd killed her, but then she shifted position. He turned back to his parents. They were looking straight at him.

They could see him! Jake felt tears of joy spring to his eyes.

His mother frowned. "Jake?"

"It's me, Mom."

She rubbed her head and winced. "Yes, I know. What's the matter? You look ill. Perhaps you should go to bed early tonight."

Jake was speechless. He'd done it. Something had *finally* gone his way. This was his first real victory!

Jake had spent the rest of the evening sitting with them as they watched the film. Such a trivial thing felt like the best time of his life. Nobody seemed aware of the time that had passed, which suited Jake fine. He wouldn't have to come up with any lies.

Things got a little dicey when his dad noticed that Jake's room was empty. Luckily he assumed it was the same thieves who had stolen Beth's laptop, and immediately called the police.

While he was on the phone, Jake's cell vibrated. He moved into the kitchen to answer it.

"Hunter? Where are you?"

Jake recognized Mr. Grimm's voice. "I'm at home. Listen, I have some great news—"

A portal suddenly opened right next to him. Mr. Grimm's hand pulled him inside.

Jake was back at the castle. The portal vanished behind him.

"What are you doing?"

Grimm hung up the phone. "Saving you! The moment your father called the police, a squad of Enforcers sprang into action. If you have reverted Psych's influence on them, then they will be able to see the task force that is about to storm your house."

Jake was alarmed. "I have to go back! Save them!"

"No. The Enforcers will not harm them. But you can't go back there. The Enforcers will always be waiting."

Jake was crushed. After everything he had been through to be with his family, his prize was spending just a few hours with them watching some awful movie!

"We can move them. How about bringing them here?"

Mr. Grimm shook his head. He looked weary, as though he had been through a battle. "This place is no longer safe. If Chameleon tracked you down here, others will too."

"Then what can I do?"

Mr. Grimm hesitated for a moment. "You have a choice. With all your powers and abilities you could really be somebody. Shape the world. Or . . . you could try to be a normal boy once again. Then nobody would be looking for you. You would have robbed both sides of their superweapon."

Jake pondered that. If he was normal again, then he could stay with his family, see Lorna, be an average kid. Would he really miss having his powers? Conversely, if he kept the powers then he could defeat those after him, and still be with his family. But he would always be addicted, a slave to Villain.net.

"If I wanted to be normal and get rid of my powers, how could I do it?"

"I have an idea. But it's a long shot. There has been a new turn of events. You may have an unexpected ally, although he doesn't know it yet."

Jake felt a jolt of excitement. "Who?"

Mr. Grimm looked uncomfortable. "This is a delicate situation, Hunter. As you are learning, the world is a complicated place. Not everything is black-and-white. Sometimes you have to turn your enemies into your friends."

"I don't understand."

"The final decision is yours to make: power and glory, or stability and normalcy. What I am about to tell you is highly sensitive for both of us. You must tread carefully."

"I don't think things can get any more mixed up than they are right now."

Mr. Grimm steepled his fingers under his chin. His black eyes seemed to bore straight into Jake.

"I assure you, they *will*."

Jake closed his eyes and calmed himself. He was about to walk into an entirely new world of trouble. He rested a hand on the door handle and hesitated. Beyond was a possible answer to rid him of his addiction.

And it was going to be *far* from easy to deal with. He opened the door and entered.

"Jake!" Lorna Wilkinson turned in surprise, a smile stretching across her face. "What are you doing here?"

"I heard there'd been an accident," said Jake. He hoped he was acting convincingly. "I just had to see you. Make sure you were okay."

He crossed the room and hugged Lorna tightly. His mouth felt dry. The one person he had extended his feelings to had turned out to be a real dark horse.

She was a superhero. Mr. Grimm had told him *everything*.

Jake looked around the room. "Hi, Toby. And you're Emily, right?"

Lorna's brother, Toby, and her friend Emily both nodded, their brows knitted with suspicion.

"I think I better explain," Jake said with a smile. "Lorna and I have been . . . sort of dating."

Expect the Unexpected

Toby looked like he'd just been slapped. He looked at Lorna, aghast.

"*He's* your boyfriend?"

Lorna blushed, and kept her arm around Jake's waist. "Yeah. He is."

Jake grinned, although inside he felt like hitting them all with a radioactive blast. They were heroes, *friends* of Chameleon—which automatically made them his enemies.

And Lorna . . . well, that was complicated.

He looked at the patient lying in bed, hooked up to an armada of machinery.

"How's the Profes—sorry, Pete?"

"Why would you care?" growled Toby.

"A friend of Lorna's is now a friend of mine. I may have been a little short with him, but if he's really hurt . . . "

"What *exactly* did you hear?" Toby asked suspiciously. "This is a private hospital."

"Heard he was hit by a truck. I went to your house earlier to see Lorna," Jake said, recalling the excuse Grimm had armed him with. "There was some guy there called Mr. Grimm. He told me where to find you."

Toby nodded, apparently satisfied.

"Yeah. A truck. He's not in very good shape."

Jake stared at the boy in the bed. Pete Kendall had been his favorite bullying target back at school. A real wimp who never fought back. And now it appeared that he had been one of Hero.com's foot soldiers. Jake recalled when he'd last seen the Professor at school. It was when Knuckles had been pounded into a bunch of cars. Jake had originally thought that it was because Chameleon was on his tail, but now he realized it was the Professor who had attacked Knuckles.

"Hope he pulls through," Jake said earnestly.

According to Grimm, Pete had fought a huge battle with Basilisk at the Foundation's secret headquarters. Jake didn't believe it, until Grimm showed him security footage of the event. As he had watched the two figures fight on screen, Jake started to respect the nerd he had been bullying for years.

During the fight Pete had smashed through numerous vats of superpowers, exposing himself to higher dosages than Jake had ever been subjected to. Then he'd fallen into a coma. Nobody knew what the effects of absorbing *so much* superpower, so quickly, would be, and the only benchmark they had was what had happened to Jake.

Jake's DNA was entangled with the whole Villain.net system, but Pete had no such issues. Only when he recovered would they truly know how he had changed.

The solution to Jake's final problem lay inside the victim of his most aggressive bullying.

* * *

Expect the Unexpected

Jake excused himself from the hospital as soon as he could. He had wanted to see the evidence with his own eyes. He had also wanted to see Lorna, somebody he had once liked and trusted but who had turned out to be the enemy. Luckily she knew nothing about him and Villain.net, a fact he could manipulate at a later date.

Jake crossed the dark hospital grounds to the cover of a small wood from where he intended to teleport back to the castle. He would try to see his family tomorrow, and give them a plausible explanation of why he had disappeared and heavily armed soldiers had stormed the house.

His thoughts were turbulent once again. Then he heard his name being called. He stopped. Had he imagined it?

"Hunter," came the whisper in the darkness.

The voice was behind him. He spun around—and came face-to-face with Chromosome. She leaned against a tree, not a hair out of place, and smiled warmly at him.

"You're such an easy man to follow, Hunter."

Jake smirked. "Follow me now!"

He closed his eyes to teleport—but nothing happened. He looked around in panic.

Chromosome laughed. "Sorry to have to take that power away, but I couldn't have you vanishing again before we resolved our differences."

Jake's heart sank. He couldn't fight her alone. He knew that just a few hundred yards away sat three superheroes who could help him out . . . but that meant revealing his true colors to them.

"I'm not helping you," snarled Jake. He clenched his fists and they burst into brilliant blue flames. "I'll strike you down so hard . . . "

He trailed off. Chromosome was no longer looking at him. She was staring wide-eyed behind him. Jake sensed movement and turned to see a little girl staring levelly at him.

"Kid, get out of here! Run!" Jake urged her.

"I think not, Hunter."

There was an edge in her voice that instantly alarmed Jake.

"How do you know my name? Who are you?"

"Yohg-Shuggor, the Destroyer of Worlds, the Bringer of the Night, the Spawn of the Damned, Eater of the Dead, the Apocalypse Harbinger, and the Shaker of Worlds. But you can call me Amy."

Jake backed away from the crazy kid. Then there was more movement in the shadows. It was difficult to make out features in the dim light, but he heard Chromosome gasp as six newcomers surrounded them both. Jake discovered that he was standing back-to-back with Chromosome.

"Who are you?" he demanded, sounding much braver than he felt.

"I am Necros, leader of the Council of Evil."

Expect the Unexpected

Jake shivered at the despair in the voice. He glanced at the shadowy figures circling him. Their forms were mostly hidden, but there was no escaping the sense of immense power that came from them.

There was *no* way out of this situation. He was going to die.

"Finally we catch up with you," hissed Necros. "You thought if you tried to overthrow the Council of Evil, that the Council Memberss would not hunt you down?"

"It wasn't me. It was Basilisk," Jake stammered before he realized that they were addressing Chromosome.

"This has all been a misunderstanding, Necros. A plot to remove *me* from the Council."

Jake could hear her voice tremble. He slowly moved away from her.

"Then it has succeeded. You *will* be banished!"

"No, you can't do that to me!" Chromosome screamed as the seven circling figures each raised a hand and pointed at her in unison.

Jake saw gossamer threads stream from their fingers and smother Chromosome. They quickly wrapped around her before she could struggle. Then she began to disintegrate, her body collapsing from head to foot as though she'd been turned to sand. The thin threads fell to the floor, eating away the fine dust until nothing remained.

It had been a swift execution. Her blood-curdling screams still rang in Jake's ears. He lowered his hands, the flames extinguishing. He knew it was pointless trying to fight his way out. The seven most powerful supervillains on the planet were studying him, but he could only see silhouettes and glowing eyes, and smell something like rotting meat.

"We have been searching for you too, Hunter."

"Yeah, I heard about that. So you found me. You going to kill me too?"

He just hoped it would be quick and painless. The Council members broke into laughter around him. It sounded just as bad as Chromosome's wailing.

"Kill you? You labor under a misapprehension," hissed Necros. "Why would we want to kill somebody so unique? So special? No, Jake Hunter. We sought you out because it appears we have a vacant place on the Council of Evil."

Jake was silent. This was the *last* thing he'd been expecting.

"Me?"

"Yes. We are offering Chromosome's place to you. To join the Council so that you can grow to understand your condition, powers, and potential. I guarantee that a place at the Council will ensure *all* your hopes and desires come to pass. We want you, the Dark Hunter, to join us and reign supreme."

Expect the Unexpected

Jake was surrounded, and he was facing death—but he was also being made an unbelievable offer.

A once in a lifetime offer, *literally*.

He hesitated, remembering Grimm's words: power and glory or stability and normalcy. He'd gotten his family back. Now to be with them, he just had to make a decision.

Surely he would be a fool to turn the offer down?

0
1
1
0
1
0
0
0
0
1
1
0
0
1
0
1
0
1
0
1
1
1
0
0
1
0
0
1
0
1

Andy Briggs was born in Liverpool, England. Having endured many careers, ranging from pizza delivery and running his own multimedia company to teaching IT and filmmaking (though not all at the same time), he eventually remembered the constant encouragement he had received at an early age about his writing. That led him to launch himself on a poor, unsuspecting Hollywood. In between having fun writing movie scripts, Andy now has far too much fun writing novels.

He lives in a secret lair somewhere in the southeast of England——attempting to work despite his two crazy cats. His claims about possessing superpowers may be somewhat exaggerated. . . .

Done fighting on the side of treachery and evil?

Want to get in touch with your heroic side?

Luckily, Andy Briggs, the evil genius behind DARK HUNTER, has a heroic side too. Join him in the struggle for justice in:

HERO.COM

Virus
Attack

Turn the page for a teaser chapter, and prepare to find your inner superhero!

All in a Day's Work

The rusted bow of a battered cargo vessel churned through the ocean, its destination a sliver of land on the horizon. Faded lettering on the dented bow revealed the ship's name: The *Watchman*. It moved with no running lights on, making it a black whale cutting through the sea. Dense smoke poured from its weatherworn funnel, but otherwise the vessel looked abandoned. At first glance, no one would have suspected that the crew were all ruthless smugglers, armed with automatic weapons and not a conscience among them.

They were being tracked by three superheroes silently flying above. The heroes were all thinking the same thing—the automatic weapons below were nowhere near as dangerous as the fact that they were out way past their parents' curfews. The consequences of that were too dire to contemplate.

Toby squinted, trying to make out more detail on the boat. He regretted not having tried to download some kind of night-vision power from Hero.com. But then again, he'd had no idea they would be out so late—plus he wasn't sure what the stick-figure icon for it would be. He just hoped none of them had downloaded any useless powers, as they sometimes did.

Lorna and Emily flew close on either side, talking in low voices.

"I'm getting cold," complained Lorna. Having learned from previous adventures, they were all dressed in thick black clothes, but the chill still permeated.

Toby didn't bother replying. Over the last few weeks his sister's complaints had increased with each job they had downloaded from Hero.com. His best friend, Pete, had even started to agree with her, which wasn't good news. Luckily Pete wasn't within earshot. Toby glanced around, suddenly aware that his friend had been gone longer than he'd anticipated. He glanced at the lights on the horizon.

"We're running out of time," he warned. "We can't wait for Pete. We have to stop this thing now."

"It's a massive boat. How are we supposed to stop it?" said Emily.

"Why bother? This is something we should leave for the police," Lorna grumbled.

"Police don't patrol out here," Toby snapped back.

"The coast guard, or customs, or border patrol or whatever you call it. What's the point in having these great powers if we're just stopping *normal* people?

All in a Day's Work

What about the supervillains out there? We're supposed to be fighting *them*."

Toby rolled his eyes. "It was on the job board and it needed to be done."

The list of jobs on Hero.com seemed to be growing by the day, although not every job was a direct result of an errant supervillain. "Besides, I thought we decided after the trouble with Doc Tempest that we should take things a little easier?"

"*You* decided, Toby," Lorna retorted.

Emily tried to avoid getting involved with the argument. Which was just as well, as she detected movement on the deck below. Figures had left a cabin and were running to the bow of the ship. The moonlight glinted tellingly off the rifles they carried in both hands.

"Shush, you two! Look, they're coming out!" she said—maybe a little too loudly. One of the figures looked up and began yelling in Spanish. He pointed at the three figures with the barrel of his rifle.

Toby realized with dread that, while arguing, they had moved so that the moon was *behind* them—highlighting their silhouettes so the men below could easily spot them.

"Down!" he yelled.

They all plummeted just as the dull clatter of gunfire broke out across the deck. Bullets shrieked through the air—too close for comfort.

Toby dived straight for the ocean's surface, aware that he hadn't downloaded any power that would render him bulletproof. He was so low that foam from the boat's wake soaked his chest. He glanced up to see that Lorna had thrown up a protective shield of energy that rippled as bullets harmlessly struck it. Emily cowered close behind her. *Typical of Lorna to pick a defensive power*, thought Toby. Not that selecting powers on Hero.com was a straightforward process.

Chameleon, the only heroic Prime that Toby had ever met, had told them there was an instruction manual on the Web site. When he'd eventually found it, Toby had been baffled by the complex jargon used. He did learn that the stick figure icons, which represented the powers, were laid out with *some* degree of logic. Lorna always seemed smart enough to pick the most useful powers for their missions, whereas he just chose the most fun-looking ones.

His thoughts were interrupted as a deckhand leaned over the gunwale of the ship and spotted him. Toby could make out the square night-vision goggles the man wore. The muzzle flash of the weapon flickered and a stream of bullets zipped past him.

Time to end this, he thought.

Toby barrel-rolled to one side to make himself less of a target. He extended his hands and fine black tendrils shot from his fingertips, each no wider than a strand of

All in a Day's Work

cotton, but bunched together they were as thick as rope. The sticky tendrils splattered against the man's night-vision goggles and the gun. Toby yanked the strands back, tearing the equipment from him. He shook his hands and the strands broke away, falling into the sea. The startled man stared in Toby's direction as if he'd just seen a ghost, then spun around and ran across the deck, shouting in panic.

Above, Emily peeked around Lorna's energy shield and flicked her hands. A pair of golden orbs, no bigger than Ping-Pong balls, sprang from her palms and raced toward the crew. She watched in fascination as the heat-seeking orbs were guided toward two men, striking them in the chest. The orbs exploded with a dull *plop* and the men were catapulted across the deck. They slammed into the bulkhead, weapons skittering away.

A third man gaped as his colleagues were blown aside, and then looked up as if realizing for the first time that the two girls were suspended in the air as if by magic. He hesitated in firing—giving Emily an opportunity to fire another set of golden orbs.

The man dropped his weapon and fled. He glanced behind him to see the orbs were weaving across the deck in his direction. He skidded around a corner leading to the main cabins and checked behind him. The orbs were relentlessly pursuing. He increased his pace and threw himself into an open cabin door, pushing his whole body against the steel door to close it.

Both orbs hit the door with such thunderous force that the metal buckled and the door was blasted from its hinges. The warped steel propelled the man across the cabin and into the far wall, knocking him unconscious.

Toby gained altitude to join Emily and Lorna.

"I thought there would be more of them," said Toby. "And I thought pirates would be a lot tougher."

"Wrong type of pirates," said Lorna in her best "ye olde pirate" accent.

"It's turning!" exclaimed Emily. As they watched, the boat increased speed and began to slide in the water. "Must be somebody at the wheel."

Toby felt slightly disappointed at what seemed like an easy victory—he had been expecting the mission to be a lot more fun, but knew better than to say so out loud. "We didn't need Pete after all, the slacker. Let's get onto the boat and stop it."

Toby wondered if Pete was okay. The last time he'd seen him was when Pete had plummeted underwater several minutes ago, convinced he had downloaded aquatic powers. Toby wasn't too concerned, since Pete was a strong swimmer. Besides, his friend had been acting differently since they had been using the superpowers. Toby just hoped being a hero wasn't going to his head, like it was with his sister.

All in a Day's Work

They edged forward toward the ship's dark helm at the front of the boat. As they drew nearer they could see the captain inside the control room, bathed in pale lights. The captain didn't look around, but instead stared at his instruments. The ship was old enough to be steered by a large wheel, instead of the small computer joysticks of modern vessels. The captain was using all his weight to keep the wheel level.

Toby landed on the raised deck and took a step forward when Lorna suddenly gave a loud yelp. She had been about to follow her brother through the control room door when she was violently dragged up and backward into the sky by some invisible force. She suddenly stopped and hung stationary for a second, before rapidly zigzagging through the air like a balloon—coming to another abrupt halt. She stopped screaming for a microsecond before plummeting into the water.

Lorna's screams alerted the captain. He spun around to see Toby—who had his back to the man, watching his sister's plight. He didn't see the captain pick up a small fire extinguisher and raise it to strike Toby's head.

Emily dragged her gaze from Lorna, who was thrashing in the ocean, to Toby, who was about to be clocked by the captain.

"Tobe!" she screamed and extended her hands. The orbs appeared as before—but then they popped like harmless soap bubbles. For a brief second she panicked—the friends' powers were only temporary and liable to run out at any moment. But she reasoned that her powers hadn't expired, or else she wouldn't still be flying.

Toby heard her warning and turned just as the captain swung the fire extinguisher down. Toby ducked aside but the extinguisher still clipped his shoulder. The might of the attack forced him to the floor, his right arm numb from where he'd been struck. The captain loomed over him and hissed in an unfamiliar language. Toby could see the bloodthirsty rage in the man's eyes. . . .

A sound like a million waterfalls rumbling interrupted the captain. After years on the sea, he knew trouble from the ocean when he heard it. He looked through the control room's window. Toby followed the captain's gaze, his eyes widening.

A wall of water rose in front of the ship, almost one hundred feet tall and four times as wide. It was a tidal wave—except this one didn't move, but stood up from the sea like a liquid wall, seawater rising on one side and cascading down the other. The cap of the wave bubbled and frothed, betraying the force of the water contained beneath—and Pete stood on top of it like a champion surfer. Dressed in his black wetsuit with his arms folded, he was laughing in delight.

Log on for your own superadventure at:

www.heroorvillainbooks.com

Test yourself to find out if
you're a hero or a villain

Create your own avatar—choose
powers, costumes, and more!

Challenge your friends to
a live fight

Learn more about the books

Watch the book trailers

Meet Andy Briggs and watch
his video blog

Superpowers are just a click away. . . .